C000154170

Going for GOLD

Providence Gold Series - Book Four

MARY B. MOORE

Copyright © 2019 Mary B Moore

All rights reserved

No part of this book may be reproduced, copied or transmitted in any form or by any means, electronic or mechanical, including photocopying, recording, or by any information storage or retrieval system without written expressed permission from the author, except in the case of brief quotations embodied in critical articles or reviews. This is a work of fiction. All names, characters, businesses, places, events and incident are products of the authors imagination and are used fictitiously. Any resemblance to actual persons, living or dead, events or locales is purely coincidental.

Cover design: Tracie Douglas https://www.facebook.com/darkwatercovers/

Cover Photograph: Deposit Photos

Editor: B&C

The use of actors, artists, movies, TV Shows, and song titles/ lyrics throughout this book are done so for storytelling purposes and should in no way be seen as advertisement. Trademark names are used in an editorial fashion with no intention of infringement of the respective owner's trademark.

This book is licensed for your personal enjoyment. This book may not be re-sold or given away to other people. If you would like to share this book with another person, please purchase an additional copy for each recipient. If you are reading this book and did not purchase it, or if it was not purchased for use only, then you should return it to the seller and please purchase your own copy.

All rights reserved. Except as permitted under the Copyright Act 1911 and the Copyright Act 1988, no part of this publication may be reproduced, distributed, or transmitted in any form or by any means, or stored in a database or retrieval system, without the prior express, written consent of the author.

This book is intended for mature adults only and contains consensual sexual content and language that may offend some. Suggested reading audience is 18 years or older. I consider this book as Adult Romance. If this isn't your type of book, then please don't purchase it.

This book is covered under the United Kingdom's Copyright Laws. For more information on the Copyright, please visit: https://www.gov.uk/copyright/overview.

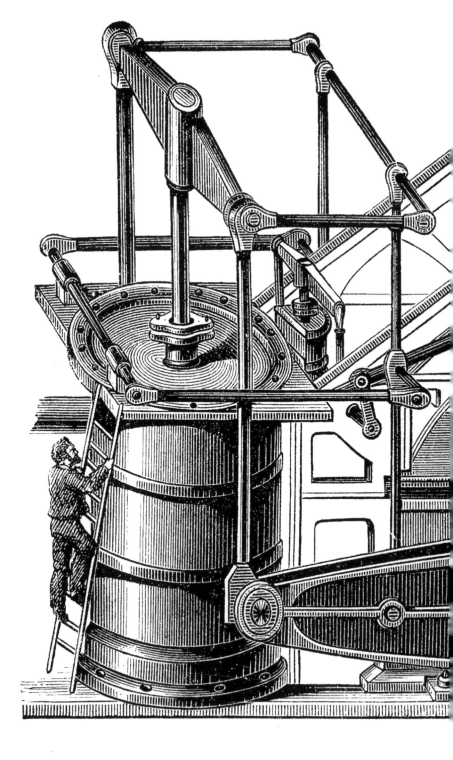

GOING FOR GOLD

Charlotte

Two years ago, my life changed. All it took was a lot of alcohol, mainly tequila, and my friend's fortune telling grandmother reading my future.

Now, I count the minutes I waste and keep them in a document on my phone, tallying up them all up. I just know I'm going to feel bitter over those wasted minutes. I've also started working through my bucket list, adamant I'll get through it all. Why? Because I'm twenty-one, the age she said life would change for me at.

And then I meet Levi Townsend, the man who shoots my minute tally to an insane level. I'm not sure if this pisses me off, or if I like that he tests my limits.

Does it even matter though? Not with the big day coming soon.

I just need to get through all the items on my list before the big day comes.

Levi

Who the hell believes in that fortune telling crap? Oh, she does!

It's just my luck that the woman I keep bumping into and can't get out of my head is convinced she's jinxed, and measures every minute of her day like it's her last.

Then again, maybe it is?

Being a Townsend, I'm going to test her self-control, push her boundaries, drive her crazy… and I can't wait.

But, what happens when it turns from 'just fun between friends' to 'this isn't friendship, it's freaking love'? I'll repeat – I. Am. A. Townsend. We're determined, we're loyal, we're honest, we love deeply and we'll drive you out of your ever-loving mind until you say 'yes'.

So, I'll just have to change her mind!

DEDICATION

I'm so sorry I had to delay Levi by two weeks, but he's finally here. I have to say, I think he ties with Cole on being my favorite Townsend ever (sorry Tate!).

As 2019 draws to an end, it's been a huge year for me – both with writing and in my personal life. This will be the 8th book I've written this year, 10th I've published (including the Providence box sets), and my 21st book all together (with one that isn't live anymore because it was for an anthology). I want to thank all of you for your support, for loving the Cheap Thrills and Providence Gold series, and for just being the best supporters ever. When I first started writing, I figured that I'd get maybe five readers maximum. Over the last almost four years, that figure has been blown out of the water, but this last year has been the most surreal one. So many of you have read and loved the Townsends and Cheap Thrills crazies and reached out to me, and there really are no words to describe how amazing that feels.

When I read over Going For Gold, I could see how distracted I'd been as I was writing it. My son hasn't had an easy year health wise, and looking after him and writing Levi... something suffered. So, delaying it to rewrite the whole thing was a horrible decision to make, but I'm hoping I did him justice for you all. Let it never be said that Mary delivered a sub-par Townsend, damn it.

So, thank you, and this one is dedicated to the Townsend lovers.

M xox

PS read the note that follows after the book. Trust me, there's some news in there you'll like x

CHAPTER ONE

Charlotte

I t felt like my hair was being pulled out of my head as I looked down through the clouds at the ground – a really fucking hard ground. I mean, I've walked on it since I was thirteen months old, I knew how hard it was, and the distance between my body and it right now wasn't really compatible with me being a breathing and living human being. All it would take is the parachute failing, a flock of birds ripping through the thin fabric, being off by one second when the cord was pulled… I was too young to die.

Turning to look at the asshole beside me whose fault this all was, I opened and closed my mouth a couple of times, trying to figure out exactly what I wanted to say. Thankfully, he wasn't aware of me doing this seeing as how he was still looking down at where I'd just looked up from.

Here's the thing – I said I wanted to cross items off my bucket list, but I hadn't really known what I'd wanted to do. Out of desperation, I'd gone online and done an internet search for bucket list items. Surprisingly, skydiving was number one on most of the lists. The reason it was surprising was because it meant that thousands of people around the world were listing things they wanted to do before they died, and number one was something that would kill them outright.

When Levi had told me his brother Noah was into jumping out of planes like a psycho kamikaze, I'd asked him about it, but he'd made it seem easy like jumping off a swing – the lying asshole of a bull. Yeah, he was the asshole of a bull, the tail end of the angry bovine creature with horns on its head. I wasn't going to go into how crusty one of those would be, not with my stupid decisions staring me in the fact at that precise moment, anyway.

As soon as I found my way out of this mess, I was going to cause him pain. Then I was going to have another look at my list and take off things that might bring me death, especially as I was trying to get through all of this just in case that was what was coming to me. I should have gone for jumping into a pit of feathers, or lying in a room with puppies crawling over me – which, FYI, wasn't on any of the bucket lists online, but it totally fucking should have been.

A hard tap to the shoulder almost made me embarrass myself.

"Are you ready, Charlotte?" Lucifer – or Pete if you went by what his parents had called him – yelled over the sound of the air rushing in around us.

I was still facing toward Levi, so I saw the guy attached to him doing the same thing. I'd never been the type who prayed, but I figured now was the best time to start.

Please, God, don't let him say yes. Let him back out of it so that I've got a good reason to do the same thing.

"Charlotte?" Pete yelled, giving my arm a shake.

Just then, Levi and his guy scooted to the open edge of the

plane and started preparing to jump. It was like I was watching it happen in slow motion now, and I was vaguely aware of a dark tunnel creeping in around my vision as they started to lean out of the side of the plane. That's when something constricted around my chest, and I started panting, doing my best to get oxygen into lungs that felt like they were the size of a quarter as the tunnel closed in more quickly.

Just as they'd leaned past the point of return, the tunnel won and it was lights out. The last thing I heard as I slipped into the darkness, was Levi yelling, *"I've changed my mind!"*

Or, at least that's what I thought I'd heard.

Levi

Keeping my eyes on the road, I silently seethed – yes, *seethed* – over today's events. When I'd said I'd help her fulfill her bucket list, I'd thought she meant shit like tattoos and climbing a mountain, not skydiving. I'd figured that sending her to Noah and hearing him explain exactly what happened would make her change her mind, instead she'd been even more determined to do it thanks to his pep talk.

When I got home, I was going to kill my brother, hug my best friend who was also his wife, and then kill him all over again.

"It's fun." He'd said. *"You'll love it."* He'd said. *"It's as harmless as riding a bike."* He'd said. *"You'll want to do it again, and again, and again."* He'd said.

I should have just paid attention to Luna's frantic head shaking behind him, instead of thinking that I could hack it.

And the betrayal of the woman – admittedly beautiful woman – beside me, passing out so she didn't have to do it. Granted, she couldn't have helped it, but would it have killed the guy she was attached to, to just do it? She could have woken up halfway down and still crossed it off her bucket list even though she didn't actually do the jumping. Or I could have had the best photos of her passed out a million miles above the ground – and those photos would have been awesome. But no, she had to pass out and wake up as the plane was coming into land, while I plummeted to my death with a dude's dick pressed against my ass.

Awe-fucking-some.

"We should discuss what happened," Charlotte whispered, but I stayed quiet. When she realized I wasn't going to say anything, she added, "It was an accident." Still, I stayed silent. "Was it at least fun?"

That snapped me out of my brush with death snit. "Fun? Fun is when you enjoy something, when you smile and feel light because it's been something thrilling. Know what isn't fun?" I swear to God her lips twitched, so I pulled over to the side of the road so that I could blast her with my expression – my fierce and terrifying expression as a survivor.

Cutting the engine, I angled in my chair so that I was looking at her now. "Fun isn't feeling your brain travel from your head, through your body, and out of your ass hole. Fun isn't realizing that when that cord is pulled, the parachute may very well fail…"

"They said you had a backup parachute," she interrupted, but I was too far in to even try to listen to her attempt at being reasonable.

"Fun isn't realizing that your last moments before you hit the ground and your feet take the opposite direction your brain took – going up through your ass, into your now empty skull – were going to be spent with the dick and balls of the guy you're strapped to against the crack of your ass," I hissed, leaning forward as far as my seatbelt would let me.

Her breath hitched, and for a second I felt really bad about ranting, and thought that maybe I'd scared or upset her… until she choked out, "You could really feel his wiener and nuts against your ass crack?" When I just glared at her, she took a shuddering breath in. "Did he at least give you his number before we left?"

Hitting my hand down on the button to undo my belt, I threw it over my shoulder, not even wincing when it hit the window, and moved until our noses were an inch apart. "You left me to die."

"I think you're being a tad dramatic, Levi. You were attached to a good-looking dude who knew what he was doing. And, if you think of it in a positive way, he was well hung enough for you to feel it through his clothing against your ass."

All I heard through the pounding in my head was a bunch of apologies and sweet words, though, and they weren't going to help her. "Don't try to sweet talk your way out of this…"

Frowning, she tilted her head to the side and looked at me. "I wasn't sweet talking my way out of it. I was pointing out how fortunate you were…"

I shook my head as I held my hand up. "Stop begging, it's not going to work," I said firmly, and then proceeded to list the reasons why. I'd only gotten halfway through the first one when I realized I was starting to slur my words and heard her saying something through the roaring in my head.

"…yeah, he's slurring and talking weird," she said, and then suddenly I was being blinded by the light going on. "Shit, it looks like he's in shock." I tried to get my mouth to move, but it felt like my tongue was ten sizes too big for it. Maybe I was allergic to skydiving? "Ok, get Parker to meet us there."

And that was kind of it for me. I was still conscious but

nothing would work how I wanted it to, which is how I found myself half on the passenger seat of my car, and half on the floor of it.

"Don't worry, I'll have you home soon," the sweet voice of an angel reassured me as I fell sideways into the door. "Oops, sorry," it muttered, and then I was being thrown about the place like we were driving over Lego. My teeth rattled, my bones played the ultimate game of Jenga inside my body, and the limits of my bladder were tested.

After what felt like a lifetime of the shaking and rattling, it finally stopped, and my head fell backward on my neck as the world just switched off. Now why couldn't it have done that while I was on the plane?

CHAPTER TWO

Charlotte

I was a nurse, and nurses knew what to do when things like this happened, right? Sure, but if there was a doctor around that was even better - and I was definitely leaving it up to the doctor.

"Stop pacing," Ariana sighed, stretching her legs out in front of her. "You heard what the donkey dick said – Levi's just fine," she reminded me, and then added, "he's a big pussy, but he's just fine."

I'd never been a superstitious person – well, up until I went to that damn party two years ago, that was. Now I found myself doing the stupidest things like throwing salt over my shoulder whenever it tipped over, or doing something else to erase bad luck whenever something like that happened. All the sites on my phone and laptop were open to subjects based on luck, old fables, and things like that, because I just wasn't willing to take chances now. Well, with the exception of jumping out of a plane, obviously.

Judge away, whatever you want to do, but I was doing what I needed to do. I had a notebook full of good luck actions and omens, and I had another one with things that led to bad luck or warned of bad things about to happen. I didn't look at these ones as often as I did at the beginning now, though, after Levi started doing my bucket list items with me. He'd read through these two at the same time and had told me, "All this constant bad and good luck shit stops now. No more throwing salt and being scared of life."

He didn't know the story, but apparently if you live your life like something bad will happen at any second, you won't enjoy life - and the whole purpose of a bucket list was to enjoy life, right? So they were in a drawer now, and I only did a couple of items from them every now and then.

Then there was my third notebook with items for my bucket list. Well, I had two other notebooks, seeing as how I technically had two bucket lists. Bucket list one: the normal things. Things that were exciting and could be done in public.

Bucket list two: sex related things that I wanted to try. Item number one on it was to have sex, the rest were notes from online searches (again), porn, and from looking at things I'd found in sex shop sites online.

I wasn't brave enough to try a majority of the two small pages worth of things, but my theory was - if others enjoyed them enough to buy the toys and do it in porn, then I should open myself up to trying them. In safety of my mind, that theory totally worked. Not surprisingly, the second one was hidden under my pillow and never left my home, but I took the first one with me everywhere so that I could add to it whenever something hit me.

How did I turn into this person who was looking at every minute like it may well be their last? Well, I wasn't at that stage – I was at the 'what if' stage. What if something happened, and I hadn't experienced as much as I could? Well, I'd end up sitting on my cloud, looking down on the world at everyone having fun and would most likely be pissed at the missed opportunities. I'd be like one of those spirits on a television show that wouldn't cross over to the other side, begging people to let me hijack their bodies so I could just do what I needed to do, and I just didn't want to be that spirit.

Sound dramatic? Well, let me rewind to the moment that led up to me becoming this person. Two years ago at my friend Amber's birthday party, she'd brought in this familiar looking old woman and told us that we were all getting our 'futures read'. The woman turned out to be her grandmother, and she'd made a big deal about how qualified the woman was, that she'd read the futures of celebrities and how big an honor it was for us to have her with us.

I was only nineteen, and we'd been drinking alcohol that we'd all stolen from our parents, but something about it just seemed off to me. I mean - not to mock what some people truly believed in - I found it hard to believe that someone's future or destiny could be told by reading cards, tea leaves, the lines on their palms, or whatever else was being used to do it. It didn't make any sense to me.

Regardless, I was the fifth person who was taken into the small room, and Amber's grandmother laid out five cards in front of me, studied them, and then gasped and grabbed my hand to look at my palm. That's when she laid it all out for me.

The first thing I was told was to be careful of the men in my life that I trusted. The second was that I would face heartache. The third was two people I trusted were keeping a life altering secret from me. The fourth, I would move hundreds of miles away from my hometown in Oregon in the near future. The fifth on was the most crushing, apparently my life would change after I turned twenty-one, and she said I was to make the most of the time I had left. As if it wasn't bad enough already, she said it in an almost ominous tone that made it sound sinister and all negative, not a happy, excited one, too.

Now, like I've said, I'm definitely what you'd call a sceptic about shit like this. I don't believe in ghosts, I don't believe in life after death, and I don't believe in people being able to see our futures. There's just nothing in me that finds any of it scientifically feasible, so I leave it as a matter of personal choice if people take any of that stuff seriously or not. Obviously, my feelings have changed about that now seeing as how I was picturing me being a ghost and shit, but at the time no.

Regardless, it weighed on my mind, but I didn't truly believe it and went on just living life like I normally did. I had a boyfriend named Eric who I'd known since I was middle school. He was the boy next door type of guy, and the good guy that everyone loved. We got along well and had been dating for six months by then, and it felt like it was heading for something serious. I wasn't in love, but maybe I could have gotten to that stage with him. Well, so I thought at the time.

One night, a month after the party, I came home from the library and overheard my parents arguing. This was a big deal and caught my attention because they tended to be emotionless people – ones that had pushed me all my life, but gave nothing back emotionally or physically.

Examples of that were: at age two they put me into an advanced learning pre-school. We did our alphabet, math, we learned scientific things – at *age freaking two*. After that, my parents hired a team of homeschool teachers who came over every day and worked with me on an advanced learning curriculum. Is that possible? If you have money, hell yes it is.

My parents were both leading surgeons in a hospital in

Portland that catered to rich people – celebrities, famous business moguls, the world's elite. They pioneered groundbreaking plastic surgeries and were paid huge amounts for it. Because of that of course they had the money to put their kindergarten daughter through an education at home that was years ahead of where she was meant to be.

By age eight I was in middle school. Age fifteen I graduated from high school and started college at home. Before I started, I'd decided to go into nursing, which was a huge disappointment to them. I just didn't have the mind to perform surgeries like my parents. Regardless, I stood strong, and in my second year of college I began going to classes on campus.

After school I'd go to the hospital, and I'd have to sit in surgeries and consultations with one of them. That's how it continued until I was at the stage where I could physically assist them during procedures.

I was only four months away from my twentieth birthday when I graduated and was immediately employed by my parents at the hospital they worked at. It might sound like a caring move by then, but more than likely they organized it because they were hoping I'd decide to go back and study to become what they were, aka medical robots fixated on their next paychecks.

Sound harsh? So does controlling your daughter's life to the point that the only friends she had were ones that you'd chosen for her. People you'd deemed 'suitable' to socialize with your child, people who wouldn't hinder the plan you had for them... basically, my whole life had been controlled by them to that point.

That's why I was at that party. Amber was on the approved list, my 'best friend' since I could walk, and my parents had no idea how far away she was from what they thought. She wasn't the innocent girl she made herself out to be, the one who wore the matching twin set and who was afraid of her own shadow. Amber had a dark side to her that she released through alcohol and holding parties when her parents were out of town. She was my best friend because she was the only person I was allowed to get close to until I started dating Eric.

Like I said, we'd met when I was in middle school, so when I was nine. His parents worked with mine and we were allowed to hangout now and then. It wasn't until I was almost nineteen that our relationship developed, and I was careful to hide it from my parents. We'd known each other for so long that I trusted him, I even let down the barriers and showed emotions that I didn't normally. My parents loved him as a person, but I was worried that if they'd known we were together, they'd have stopped it.

Anyway, on the night in question, I'd come home from the library preoccupied with the fact that Eric had been acting weird, and wanted to take our relationship to a new level immediately. He'd just cornered me in the library and told me to suck him off because the idea of public sex was a huge turn on for him. After that, he said he was going to fuck me over the railing that looked down onto the entrance of the building. Yes, we'd fooled around, but doing something like that was a hell no for me. I'd told him my parents were expecting me, knowing that it would make him back off, and had driven home and walked in on the argument – and every minute after that changed my life.

"THERE'S NO REASON FOR HER TO EVER KNOW," DAD YELLED, THE *sound of something slamming following it. "You were the one who forced the adoption after Kelly-Anne died, not me. I told you when I found out*

that from now on I would be in charge of what happened, and that you were never to defy me again."

A condescending laugh interrupted him. "Defy you? I think you forget who you're talking to, dear. *If it wasn't for me, you wouldn't have the reputation you have now. You wouldn't be the respected surgeon you are now. You'd be working in a city hospital, earning jack shit for your time and effort,* dear." *I heard the sound of her heels clicking on the marble floor and tensed in case she was headed toward where I was standing outside the door. "You're the one who got that girl pregnant and had to pay her off, not me. That night when she killed herself, I acted to protect our reputations. What do you think people would have said if they found out you'd had an affair? That you'd gotten the receptionist pregnant? Yet again because of me you have a good reputation, so don't you dare accuse me of 'defying' you."*

I was swallowing harshly over the lump in my throat, so I almost missed what happened next.

"At least I wanted to fuck her, Raquel," he shot back, and I heard a crack after it. "That was a cheap shot, but then that's you in a nutshell, isn't it?" My dad's voice took on a tone I'd never heard from him before. "Listen carefully, that's the only time you'll ever get to hit me. You seem to forget, dear, *I have a whole file of evidence of the shit you've done. It would be a shame if people ever saw it."*

Evidence? What kind of evidence?

"You need to stick with the plan for her, Ed. She's just graduated and is taking those damned nursing exams soon. All of that time and money for nothing because she wants to be a nurse, not a doctor. We're paying people enough to do what needs done, so she'll be re-enrolling in college to do the degree we chose for her and starting it in the fall. I've already paid for her to be accepted, just like we did before…"

"And that's the problem," he interrupted her. "All I do is pay out for her, money that's being wasted. Ten thousand dollars a month for both of them, one hundred thousand to the Dean, school fees, a car…"

I couldn't listen to anymore, so I turned around and ran out the door. I drove blindly to the one person I had left that I figured I could trust – Amber. When I got to her apartment, I let myself in with the key she'd given me, and walked in on her fucking my boyfriend as he snorted a line of white powder off her lips. They were both so high and caught up in what they were doing that they didn't even notice me standing there, or look up when the door shut behind me as I left.

It was an hour into my drive around the city that I came up with a plan. Money talked – my 'parents' had proven that tonight, so I was going to make it talk for me, too.

The next day, I went to the group of guys that I knew would be able to help me at the hospital that I'd be taking my NCLEX-RN exams at – ones that everyone was scared of apart from me – and I outlined my plan. They were good guys who were judged because of their backgrounds, and to that day I'd never even thought about them like that, so of course they asked why I wanted what I was asking for – an old car that wouldn't draw any attention. A lot of people in the area we lived in knew me and my parents, so if I was seen buying it myself, my plan would have been blown before I got the chance to leave. The guys knew I was good for the money, but they wanted to make sure I was ok.

After I gave them a brief outline of what had happened, they got me what I needed, not even accepting one hundred dollars for it in exchange for regular updates from me and the promise that I'd contact them if I was ever in trouble. See what happens when you judge people incorrectly? You miss out on the beauty that we often think doesn't exist in the world, and they almost restored my faith in humanity after the big old dump it had taken on me.

A month later I passed my exams, getting only one question wrong out of one-hundred-and-nineteen of them, and that night I climbed out of the window and got in the car the men had bought for me and left three blocks away from my house. I left a letter explaining that I knew my parent's secrets - knowing that would deter them from trying to bring me home - and drove as far away from them as I could, until I finally drove through Gonzales, and fell in love with it.

After I found a place to live, I applied for my state license and three weeks after I got it I started work at the local hospital as a registered nurse.

Initially, Eric, Amber, and even my parents called and texted, trying to get me to go home, but after I laid my cards out, threatening to report Eric to the administrator of the hospital that he'd been offered a residency at – the same hospital that my parents worked for – suggesting that they perform a drug screen on him, and threats that I knew would hit the other three hard, they stopped, and I hadn't heard from them since.

DURING THE DRIVE FROM PORTLAND TO TEXAS I'D remembered the words of the lady who'd told me my fortune at the party – be careful of the men in my life that I trusted. Given that both Eric and my father had lied to me in the worst ways, this was true.

The fact that I would face heartache was blatantly true, too. How much more can a heart break hearing out loud that your parents didn't want you, that you were adopted by one of them because you were the product of an affair with a woman who'd died?

And then to find your boyfriend and best friend fucking each other? She'd also said two people I trusted were keeping a life altering secret from me – well, duh. How about we make that two sets of two people who were doing that – one of which were being paid?

In the fourth one, she'd said that I would move hundreds of miles away, and that was maybe an understatement seeing as how it was technically two-thousand-one-hundred-and-forty miles, but I could forgive her for phrasing it as hundreds. Maybe her cards had a boundary line or something and she could only see so far?

Basically, everything she'd told me that night had come true which didn't bode well for the fifth one. I was turning twenty-one in just over a year, and her advice had been to make the most of the time I had left because life was going to change after that.

And this was something that I'd spent hours - and still spent hours - agonizing over. Did she mean life was going to change as in I was going to die, seeing as how she'd phrased it as 'the time I had left'? Was I going to lose my legs? Get hit by a car and end up in a wheelchair for the rest of my life?

What exactly did it mean?

And that's when I made a hard choice. Everything she'd predicted had happened, it had all been true, so I was going to take her advice and live life like it was my last day. I was obviously more careful with how I lived – I crossed roads when the cars stopped, I refused to drive behind vehicles that were carrying loads that could come undone in a freak accident and impale me, I drove under the speed limit, I looked up every single superstition and good luck charm there was, and I did things that people thought brought them luck every damn day.

Some people freaked out when a black cat crossed in front of them, but not me. I just rubbed the rabbit's foot in my pocket, knocked on the piece of wood I carried in my purse, and crossed my fingers. I also followed international good luck superstitions, sweeping the dirt away from my front door every night like they do in China on New Year's Eve, and I Feng Shui'd the hell out of my house.

That was also when I started my bucket list. It started off with small things and was now moving onto much bigger things the further into twenty-one I got. Initially, it had been ear piercing, four small tattoos of good luck symbols, watching Bon Jovi in concert, sitting on the roof to watch the sunrise when I was afraid of heights but wanting to see it from up high… I made a list of all of it and worked through it one by one.

And then came the bigger things, ones that I was terrified of doing and was trying to talk myself into doing, anyway.

Not once, though, did I neglect a patient or become too distracted to care for them fully. I hadn't even wanted to become a nurse, I'd wanted to be a counselor for abused kids, but I'd be damned if anyone would suffer because of what I was going through. I'd worked my ass off to be a nurse and to understand what patients needed, I wouldn't ruin that because the people in my life were messed up assholes.

I'd started off in the ER when I'd gotten the job, and now I was on the Neurological Ward dealing with different areas and conditions, which was what I'd focused on during my degree. I'd read up on it, spoken to Neurologists at the hospital I'd worked in, assisted in some surgeries when I'd wanted to get away from my parents… none of it had been by the book, but that had been one perk of being the daughter of Ed and Raquel Rose.

That was why my education had slowed down slightly – because I'd been making sure while I was doing all of this that I was learning everything I could about this area of medicine. I didn't want to rush through it and then end up fucking up someone's life.

So, now I was working with patients who had neurological illnesses and traumas, and with the conditions they suffered from, any slip of my focus and concentration could lead to life changing problems. That could happen on any ward, sure, but for some reason neurosciences had always struck me as the most complex out of all of them.

I was still only just starting out in the department and the work was hard as hell, but I loved it and was studying for my neuroscience nursing exam so that I had my CNRN and could take on even more work. I already had a lot of it done, but there was no hurrying this so I was working my ass off to make sure I was confident with what I knew.

In my first week at the hospital in Gonzales County, I'd met the Townsend family when one of their girlfriends had been brought in. It had been Tate Townsend's girlfriend Lily who'd been caught in a burning building while she was heavily pregnant, so I'd met him and his brother Levi before the others. It had only been minutes before the others, but they were my introduction to the Townsends. I'd been the one assigned with helping them all that night, something that hadn't made sense until my former boss had let it slip that one of the family members had requested me specifically.

From there, a close friendship had grown between all of us, and I had friends now instead of just work acquaintances. I had a place to go for Thanksgiving, and they'd even invited me to join them for Christmas – if I was still alive by then, that was.

But in the four months that had passed, I'd gotten to know Levi the most. He was a close friend, and I spent a majority of my free time with him, hanging out, crossing off items on my list, and laughing so hard I couldn't breathe.

My feelings for him weren't just platonic, though, and that sucked because we were friends - that freaking friend zone - and he'd never given me any sign that it could ever change.

And let's not forget the what ifs - I didn't exactly have a lot of time if things between us did change. So maybe I was better to keep him friends, and if the opportunity to have sex with him ever came up, then he'd have helped me with both of my lists.

For now, I'd take anything I could to just hang around with him and enjoy the easy way he could make me laugh and live.

CHAPTER THREE

Levi

I was focused on the geological reports that I'd just received for a site we were looking at, so it wasn't until Tate said her name that I actually listened in to what he was saying. "…Charlotte. I think it's because she sees you as a science experiment or a freak of medical nature, but Lily thinks she has a crush on you."

Looking up from the graphs and printouts covering the wooden surface, I frowned over at my brother. "Why would she think I was a freak of medical nature? Y'all just told me I was a freak of nature when we were kids."

Shrugging, he tossed the apple in his hand up in the air. "Because you are."

Closing my eyes in frustration, I dropped my head down, doing my best to talk myself out of what I wanted to do badly… and failed. Without even moving my upper body, I kicked out with my right leg, clipping him in the shin with steel toe cap of my safety boot. *"Ow,* you big, fat monkey sack. What was that for?"

Fifteen months was all that separated us - with me being the younger brother - but sometimes it felt like I was ten years older than him.

It had always been that way, though, especially after I'd met my best friend Luna when we were just kids. I'd seen a vulnerable little girl, and even though I didn't know her story then, I'd known that she'd needed to be protected. I'd been way too young to take on the role by myself, but I'd done it anyway, and had also brought her into my family so they could help out. It was an unspoken agreement from day one – we knew she was going through shit at home, and we all looked out for her from that day forward.

When I'd found out the full extent of it all, it hadn't been because she'd begged me not to do anything that I hadn't ended up in prison. It had actually been the twat in front of me who'd made it all sink in when he'd asked me who would protect her like I did if I was locked up in a cell. If we'd known that her dad was going to kidnap her and put her through hell for years, though, we maybe would have said fuck it to that question and buried him in a field – and that's something I was going to have to live with for the rest of my life. She was safe now, though, happily married to my brother, and now a mom to the light in heart, my niece Jamie.

Sighing, I stood up and turned to rest my ass on the table, losing interest in the paperwork I'd been looking at. "I don't think I need to explain or justify my actions after all these years."

Shooting a glare at me, he rubbed his shin dramatically. Well, maybe not so dramatically seeing as how those steel toe caps were kind of brutal. "I'm going to show her what you've done so she can see how mean you are."

"You swap maturity levels with Rebel?"

Rebel was his newborn daughter and had been named by her mom who had the most fucked up names for her pets, and now her child. My niece's full name was Rebel Rowser Townsend – can you believe that shit? Then again, Lily also had a chicken called King Ferdinand the Chicken – aka KFC – and another one called Bojangles, who was the size of a Pterodactyl. Who names their chickens after restaurants that specialize in freaking chicken? And her dogs, those poor furry bastards, their names were just as bad.

And I knew just how to wind my brother up. "Hey, what do you think she's gonna call your next kid? Creedence Clearwater? Jumpin' Jehoshaphat?"

"I'm willing to bet big bucks it'll be Chick Fil-A or Big Mac," a voice said, making both of us jump. I don't know how he did it, but our eldest brother Archer was a sneaky bastard who had mastered the ability to appear out of thin air at a young age.

"Funny fuckers, the two of you," Tate muttered, picking his apple up and biting into it. "At least I have a woman." Unable to leave it at that, he asked smugly, "How are Charlotte and Bonnie by the way? Haven't seen them around here for…" he paused, "*ever*."

Leaning a shoulder against the wall, Archer looked coolly at him. "That's a lie, Bonnie was here last night visiting Dahlia. As you know, seeing as how you were there, too."

Doing my best to hide how tense I was over the question, I straightened my legs out in front of me, and crossed my arms over my chest. "And I know for a fact you also bumped into Charlotte yesterday, when you went to help Parker move his office around." Something which I'd been told by Parker, obviously.

Sighing, he took another large bite, and chewed slowly on it, thinking over a comeback for both of us. When he finally knew what it was, he swallowed - what was probably nothing given how long he'd taken - and then shrugged. "Yeah, but the difference is that she wasn't here to see you," he glanced at Archer, "and Charlotte didn't mention you," he directed at me. "If y'all want tips on how to get your women, all you have to do is say."

Looking over the top of his head, Archer and I just blinked at each other, not needing to ask if he was serious out loud.

"You mean by knocking her up?" A voice asked sweetly from the doorway, this time making Archer jump, too.

A smile I'd only ever seen aimed at Lily took over Tate's face as he jumped up and walked over to where she was holding their daughter, the infamous Rebel Rowser – at least, with a name like that she would be.

"Hey, baby," he greeted, giving her a soft kiss, making both of us gag. Shooting a glare over his shoulder and ignoring Lily's snort, he leaned down to his sleeping daughter. "Hey, angel face."

Now that wasn't an exaggeration. Somehow, both of my brother's daughters were angel faces, regardless of the devil spawn who'd sired them. I'd been certain that they'd be born with horns and a tail, but they looked like miniature Disney princesses. Hell, I even had a photo of Jamie holding a silver bangle over her head like a halo, taken when she was only three weeks old.

She'd been having some photos taken by a professional photographer, and I'd had the idea to get her to hold the bangle

– which I'd given to Luna for her birthday – thinking it would look cute in her tiny fist. When she'd raised her arm and bent it so her hand was over her head and the bangle had looked like a halo, phones had come out of everyone's pockets so that they could catch the moment, and the photographer had kept her finger on the button of her camera praying loudly at least one photo turned out well.

"Thought I'd come and check in on you, and it seems it's just as well I did," Lily told him, moving further into the room and passing Rebel to Archer. "Go see your uncle, baby. He needs precious loves because your daddy's an ass."

Glaring at her, Tate snapped, "Hey!" You might think it was because of the insult that had just been lobbed his way, but it was because she'd passed his daughter to his brother and not him that was the problem.

Archer turned so his shoulder blocked him when he went to reach for her. "Get your own."

"She *is* my own," he growled.

"Then don't be so selfish and learn to share."

Sitting down in the chair her husband had just vacated, Lily shook out her arms. "She might not weigh a whole lot in the grand scheme of things, but man alive my arms are aching."

"Maybe it's because of the man-sized child standing sulking behind you," I suggested, looking pointedly over her shoulder at where he was still glaring at our brother.

Following where I was looking, she called, "Tate, come and sit down and let him cuddle his niece for Pete's sake."

It's funny how a saying like 'Pete's sake' can make you cringe, isn't it? Well, that's what it made me do when she said it, remembering the guy who'd been attached to Charlotte the last time I'd seen her.

Actually, it hadn't been the *last* time I'd seen her – that was the morning after it when I'd woken up and found her sleeping next to me in my bed. I'd rolled over and tugged her closer to me and had fallen straight back to sleep. When I'd woken up, though, she'd been gone, and I hadn't heard from her since.

It had only been a couple of days, but I felt like a part of me was missing. We'd gone from sending texts regularly – and as often as we could with our jobs – to complete silence. And I didn't like it.

Fortunately, Tate was stubborn to a fault, and always had been – in fact, if I was honest, we all were – so he distracted me from my sulking.

Shooting one last glare at Archer, he turned and his face changed completely as he looked softly at his wife, before walking over and sitting down in the chair next to where she was. When that wasn't enough, he scooped her out of her chair, and lowered her into his lap, holding her close to him.

"How are you feeling?" he murmured into her hair.

It had taken all of us days to get over it the first time we'd seen him acting like this with Lily. Tate was the joker and the one who lived life to the max in the family. So seeing him soft and tender with her? Yeah, that had taken some time and a couple of shots to get our heads around.

It also hadn't helped that the first time I'd truly been an asshole in my life had been with Lily when we'd found out she was pregnant, and I'd pretty much called bullshit on it being his baby. I knew she'd forgiven me for it, but I still hadn't forgiven myself. I hadn't even gotten past the feeling that I'd let Luna down, so I was pretty sure the guilt of what I'd done to both women was going to be with me for life.

"I'm good," she mumbled, practically curling around him. "Just tired."

I knew Rebel was having issues sleeping at night - like most newborn babies - and even my brother looked exhausted just now.

"Why don't we watch her for an hour or two, and y'all go home and have a nap?" I suggested, ignoring the panicked look Archer shot me. "I'm looking over these for a while," I gestured at the paperwork, "and Archer has some calls to make to the office, so we'll be fine."

Slapping her hand over Tate's mouth as he opened it, Lily nodded eagerly. "If you're sure?" She didn't even wait for a response from us as she stood up and tugged his hand to get him to follow. "Don't taint this for me," she warned him. "Just get up, follow me, and sleep."

Giving us a last look over his shoulder as he was led out of the room, Tate went to say something – more than likely something insulting – but his wife yelled, "Move it, Townsend. Don't you dare ruin my chance to get some sleep. I'm running on the emptiest that empty can be."

Concern took over, and he jogged away from us. "Here, let me carry you, baby. And don't think you're not in trouble. I told you I'd do some of the night feeds, but you kept telling me it was ok."

"You work with heavy machinery and technical stuff every day, Tate," she mumbled, her voice only just audible the farther away from us they got. "I don't want you being so tired you get injured."

Sitting down in the chair Lily had just been in, Archer looked down at Rebel. "Aw, isn't that sickening," he cooed. "One day, when you're a grown-up girl, you can puke on them when they talk like that."

"I think she does that anyway," I pointed out, knowing it was a fact. "And she doesn't need them being all gross and shit for it to happen."

Shrugging, he looked back down at her. "What do you do for fun then, kid? Do you wanna play on my phone?" he asked, sounding hopeful as he pulled it out of his back pocket and shook it next to her.

Holding my hands out to take her from him, I rolled my eyes at how relieved he looked when he passed her over. "She's only a couple of months old, man. She doesn't play on phones yet."

"I call bullshit on that. Kids are born with the manuals of smart phones, tablets, computers in their brains nowadays."

Looking down at the baby who was watching me with what I swear was an amused look on her face, I came up with an idea. "Wanna go see the nice nurse?"

My brother started to snort and say something smart, but then an idea hit him. "Yeah, that's a great idea. We'll take her to go see Charlotte at the hospital."

Locking the door of the office, we made our way to our parent's house where there was a spare car seat for Rebel and Jamie, and then headed to see the pretty nurse.

I wasn't blind about why Archer was so enthusiastic about going – it was the first Tuesday of the month, and that meant that Bonnie was going to be there at her monthly appointment with the geneticist. She saw him every month about her atavism, and they'd do scans and blood tests for him to take back to some big college to study.

The following month, they'd discuss the results, look at other cases she'd found, and look at other parts of her genetic makeup, hoping to understand why it happened. And Archer wanted the opportunity to catch her when she couldn't run away from him, just like I was doing with Charlotte.

And what better way to get that to happen than with our beautiful niece in our arms.

Charlotte

"I don't know how you can work with him," Ariana muttered, glaring at Parker's back. "He's such a... a... wank stain."

I bit down on the corner of my lip to hide my grin as I put the Band-Aid over her 'injury'. Apparently she'd scraped it when she was trying to get into her car – and far away from the Parker in question, but we'll gloss over that – and he'd freaked out and brought her in.

He knew full well she didn't need stitches, hell she didn't even need the Steri-Strips he'd put over it to hold the wound closed. No, the truth was he was head over heels for the girl, but she had her walls built tougher than Fort Knox and he was trying to break them down.

Because of his feelings he was jumpy when it came to her safety, so his overreaction to this tiny injury was all of that rolled into one.

Feeling sorry for the guy, I pointed out, "At least he cares, Ari."

Over the months since I'd met the Townsends we'd become good friends, and I loved the girl to pieces. She was like an M&M – a crispy coating, with a soft center, and once you got through that coating you got the sweetest surprise. But don't ever forget the crispy coating because hers was reinforced.

Frowning at me, she looked around us like she was just realizing where we were. Had she hit her head, too? Parker hadn't mentioned it, but it might account for why he was acting the way he was. "What are you doing in the ER?"

"Uh, Parker brought you in, Ari. You hurt yourself," I pointed at the Band-Aid and tried to discretely check her pupils while she was looking at me.

"I know that, but you're not usually down here," she growled, and I realized what she meant.

Sighing, I crossed my arms and tried to shake off the funk I had going on. Today had been a shitty day, and on top of it I missed her brother.

I hadn't slept properly since the whole skydiving-gate thing and had only gotten a maximum of forty-five minutes sleep for the last couple of nights. I was irritated, exhausted, emotional, and hormonal.

Yup, to add insult to injury, my period had hit the morning after we'd gone skydiving, meaning that I had to run for my life or poor Levi would have woken up to a mess. Fucking joy.

"Things were quiet upstairs and they were understaffed down here, so I came to help out," I told her. "Plus, I heard that my favorite patient in the world had been brought in by her favorite doctor in the world – and who would want to miss that?"

Before she could reply, the doctor in question came back holding a disposable tray. "Ok, I've got the tetanus one ready," he said, picking the syringe up and looking over at her. "If you can…"

Jumping off the bed, she put her hands on her hips and glared at him. "If you come near me with that thing, I'll shove it up your dick."

"Whoa," I said loudly, holding my hands up in front of me. "Ok, let's settle down a bit. Ari, he's only…"

"I see we've got here just in time," a voice I recognized said behind me. "Nurse Pretty, will you please hold this little angel while we assist the good doctor?" Levi asked when I turned around, holding out a baby to me.

My arms shot out automatically, the irrational fear that he'd think they were there when they weren't hitting me, and he put a sleeping bundle of beauty in them.

Bringing her closer to my chest, I recognized her as Tate and Lily's daughter Rebel, and my heart melted. I'd been there when she came out into the world, and they'd asked me to be her godmother last week before Levi had jumped out of the plane. I wanted to do that for them and Rebel badly, even though I had some reservations given what *might* be happening to me in the near future, but there was also the chance that it could be a positive thing, so I'd said yes.

I didn't know what a godmother did, but I'd make sure I followed the instructions once I got the chance to look them up.

"I'll take heads, you take tails," a voice that I recognized as belonging to Archer this time rumbled, as he moved around me to join his brother.

Taking a step away from them, I watched as both men moved at the same time to hold Ariana in place for the vaccination. I'd expected them to just grab her arms and hold her still, but Archer wrapped his around her upper half, anchoring her own arms tightly against her body, while Levi squatted and wrapped his around her legs.

"Oh my God," she screeched, "you're not seriously doing this. I'm an adult, I get to pick and choose when I get a…" she trailed off when Parker took a step toward her and uncapped the syringe. "Swear to God, Knight, if you touch me with that, I'll…"

Oh, he touched her with it. In fact, he yanked down the side of her jeans so that part of her ass cheek was out - getting a glare from Levi, whose head was near the area that was uncovered by the move - and then stuck her with the needle.

Kissing his hand, he patted the place he'd just injected gently. "Sorry, baby. But it's better safe than sorry."

As he stepped back, Archer and Levi looked at each other nervously. "Do we release her on three?" Archer asked him, looking around where we were, like he was looking for an exit.

When he'd brought her in, Parker had put her in one of the private examination rooms, so it was a small enclosed space we were standing in. Basically, this meant they were going to have to run for their lives out the door and far away from the building because if she decided to get revenge, they didn't have much space to avoid her in.

"Uhm…" Levi hummed, copying what his brother had just done and looking around us. "I think last time we let go of the legs on two, and the top on three."

"Why do you get to run away first?"

"Because I'm the one closest to her ass. Do you know how sick this is?" Levi asked, leaning away from the area in question.

Shaking my head, I walked around the arguing brothers and the woman who was silently fuming, and stood in front of them. "Both of you release her on three," I ordered. Not giving them a chance to argue about it, I started counting. "One… two…three."

As they let go, I slid the baby into her aunt's arms, trying not to laugh when they tripped over each other as they ran out the door, leaving Parker alone in the room with us.

"Ari…" he began, but she wasn't in the mood to hear whatever he had to say.

Keeping her eyes on Rebel, she said in a cute tone, "I really wouldn't if I was you. I know where all of you live, and you've got to fall asleep at some point, so don't give me a reason to focus all of my anger on causing you pain instead of spreading it equally across the three of you." Then she added, "I'll have to see how I feel later."

And, not looking at him once, she turned and walked out, stopping only to pick up the set of car keys on the floor.

Looking over my shoulder at Parker, I was surprised to see him smiling at the empty doorway. "Damn, she's a firecracker, isn't she?"

He sounded almost proud when he said it, which confused me. "You could say that. And that's a good thing?"

Looking at me now, he grinned widely. "Yes, it is. Can you imagine living with someone who was boring? No, she's absolutely perfect." Not knowing what to say, I just nodded in agreement with him, hoping that he survived whatever it was he had planned for the two of them.

As he walked toward the doorway, he said over his shoulder, "And those were the keys to Levi's truck. With the mood she's in, I can't wait to see what she does to it."

Now that snapped me out of my funk!

CHAPTER FOUR

Levi

S o it would be an understatement to say that the trip to the hospital to see Charlotte hadn't gone as I'd expected. I hadn't gotten to speak to her, I hadn't been able to make sure we were ok, my sister was pissed off at us now, my truck was missing, and I had a sinking feeling that it was my pissed off sister who had the vehicle.

"Do we call the police?" Archer asked, looking at the compact car which was now parked in the space my truck had been in.

Scratching my chin – and making a mental note to put some beard oil on my beard after my shower tonight – I mulled it over. "Probably best not to piss her off even more by getting her arrested," I muttered. "We'll have to call Mom or Dad and see if they can come get us."

He was silent for a second, and then mumbled, "I'm not sure I want to go home. She's mean when she's pissed."

"Who's pissed," a voice asked behind us, making us both jump until we realized who it was. Actually, that was until Archer realized who it was, and turned quickly to look at her.

"Hey, Bonnie," he said softly. *Smooth!*

"Hey," she replied, and then looked at me. "Who's pissed at you?"

Here's the thing about Townsend men – we have a knack of pissing women off without meaning to. In fact, most of the time we don't even know how we did it, which is where it becomes a problem.

And standing in front of us, ignoring Archer, was the perfect example. Mind you, there was another perfect example inside the hospital right now, but I think I knew what I'd done to her, so that might not count.

"Ariana," I explained, shoving my hands in my pockets and rocking back on the heels of my boots. "We held her so that Parker could give her a tetanus shot, and now she's got my truck."

Her wince didn't put my mind at ease. Ariana had been terrified of needles since she was a baby. Every time she needed a vaccination, we'd all had to go to help hold her down for it. On the occasions when she'd needed stitches, the doctors had tried to get us to leave, and had then begged us to come back when they'd gotten a taste of her phobia.

I remembered her running past us one time, with her gown open at the back showing everyone her booty. We had to chase her around the ER for thirty-five minutes just to get five stitches above her right butt cheek.

I can't remember how she'd injured herself to begin with, but I remembered having to run with my hands over my eyes because I didn't want to see her ass again.

I'd ended up almost knocking myself out on a pillar, Tate had sprained his wrist, Archer bruised his shin on a table, Noah ended up knocking over a magazine rack and almost breaking his neck when his foot got stuck in the wire frame, and Dad went home with bruises all over his arms where she'd bitten him. Stories like that traveled, and Bonnie had obviously heard them.

"You might want to move and change your names," she suggested.

Taking a step closer to her, Archer raised her chin with the tip of his finger. "Are you ok? You look tired, Bonnie."

Blowing out a breath, she moved away from him. "Yeah, just got a lot going on. Y'all need a ride home?"

Not missing a beat, Archer nodded. "Yeah, that would be great."

Just then, the voice I wanted to hear spoke up behind me. "I'm headed that way if you want me to take them instead, honey?"

Turning around, I saw Charlotte standing there with her backpack on her shoulder. With my attention not on my niece or my sister now, I saw the dark circles under her eyes. I didn't like that she was tired or that she might not be feeling well, and my focus shifted from just needing to spend some time with her and fixing whatever it was that I'd done, to helping her get better.

Fortunately, my brother fixed the situation – for once. "I'll go with Bonnie, you go with Charlotte."

Not wanting to give her time to change her mind, I grabbed her hand and tugged her away from them.

Digging her heels in as much as she could, Charlotte tried to stop me. "Wait…"

Closing the distance between us in two steps, I wrapped my free arm around her waist and looked down into her big purple-blue eyes.

When we'd met, I'd thought she was beautiful, and I'd known she was special, but then we'd become friends and I'd assumed that was all we were ever going to be. But things change, feelings change, and I wanted us to be more than just friends.

I wasn't sure if this overwhelming need I was feeling to look after her right now was associated with it, but I needed her to be ok with me.

Leaning down so that our faces were only inches apart, I whispered, "Baby, I know you're pissed at me, and I think I know why – but I'm not certain I know why, so I might be wrong on that – but I need to spend time with you. Not speaking to you or seeing you for the last three days has been hell, and I just want to…"

"Uh, Levi," she interrupted, but her expression was definitely softer than it had been before. "I was just going to say that my car's parked over there," she pointed behind us at her small blue piece of shit car.

How I'd missed the blue banger I didn't know – well, I did, and the reason for my distraction was standing right in front of me.

"Ah, so it is."

I went to start walking toward it, but her next words stopped me mid-step. "But I've missed you as well, so maybe we can go somewhere to talk?" She spoke so softly that I wasn't sure if I'd misheard her, but I didn't care if I had.

I wasn't going to push her into anything, but I was going to start moving our relationship in a new direction. After months of bucket list items that either had me almost needing therapy, or trying to figure out what the hell kind of life she'd let that she didn't even have her ears pierced, I was going to introduce her to a whole new area of life experiences.

A relationship with a Townsend.

Charlotte

Driving while you're distracted – it's never recommended. So, how distracting is it driving with a guy who basically ticked all your boxes? The answer was very. I didn't even know I had boxes to tick, if I was honest. Yeah, I could tell you if a guy was hot or not, I'm not that basic, but to be able to list attributes that made up my perfect man? Eh, not so much. Sheltered life, sheltered mind and all that.

The first time I'd seen Levi, I'd been a bit intimidated by him and Tate. They were both tall and good looking, but they'd also been upset, angry, and stressed because of what had happened to Lily, so when they'd turned to look at me I'd taken a step back. It had only taken me all of two minutes to realize that they were good guys, and better than most, for me to drop my defenses.

Strange, right? How can you meet someone, judge them incorrectly on sight, but see straight through them in a matter of minutes? I still wasn't sure that I could answer that, but they had a way about them that you just knew they were great guys. Sure, they could still be dicks without meaning to be, but they went out of their way for people and I loved that about the family.

And I had a six-foot-three inch tall hunk of brooding Townsend currently sitting beside me in my crappy, tiny little car. Freaking distracting! If they put this in a driving test and you didn't crash, they should give you a special license – one made out of gold. Hell, maybe even a trophy to glue to the front of the car so that people could see what a great driver you were.

Needing to break the silence, I went with the first question that hit me. "So… how's the weather just now?"

The sharp rapping of big raindrops on the window and the screeching of the wipers, meant that the answer to that question was obvious. With a wince, I shuffled around in my seat, wishing I could rewind the last two minutes.

"Really?" he asked incredulously. "You want to discuss the weather?"

He had a point.

"I'm nervous. You're sitting there all…" I waved my hand at him, not taking my eyes off the road. "And I'm sitting thinking that if I had a knife I could cut the tension in this car. Like slice it finely like a sushi chef."

Nervous rambling, it makes verbal vomit come out of all of us.

As the silence stretched on, I began to drum my hands on the wheel. It probably wasn't the best idea seeing as how the car was almost being held together with tape and there was every possibility that the wheel could pop off it was that bad, but if that happened with any luck I'd be thrown from the vehicle when we crashed, and could run off into the woods to live off the land and disappear forever. Nary a Levi or a Townsend in sight to remind me of this moment. Maybe that's what the fortune chick meant?

I could live in hope.

Focusing even more on the road, I almost missed the turning onto the land where the Townsend's houses were. It wasn't a ranch or a commune and it wasn't a housing development. To be honest, I wasn't sure what they even called it, so I just called it Townsend Central.

Jerking the wheel, I took the turn onto the road that led through it, wincing when we hit a pothole and then another one a short distance away from it.

"Shit, they were meant to be fixing this," he sighed, reaching up the grab the weird handle above his head.

On the next pothole, there was a thud, and when I turned to look at him, he was staring at the handle - except now he was holding it in front of his face, when it had been attached to the vehicle only seconds before.

Did I really need to point out my car was a piece of shit to him? No, but I did anyway, making sure to phrase it as positively as possible. "This car's old. In fact, I think it's mainly running on a wing and a prayer right now. Just as well it was only the weird handle and not a door or the engine, right?"

Unfortunately, at that moment, we passed by his parent's house and the security lights turned on, lighting up the inside of the car. This meant that I could clearly see him gaping at me out of the corner of my eye, but decided to just carry on like I hadn't until we got to his house.

Pulling up, I pressed on the brakes, wincing when a metallic screech followed it. It liked to do that in wet weather… and dry weather… basically it made noises in all weather, I don't think it was picky about what exactly was going on with it.

Cutting the engine, I turned to look at him, smiling widely and waiting for him to move. I knew we needed to talk, but after that drive I felt like I had someone playing on drums inside my chest. It probably wasn't best to conduct a normal, rational, mature conversation when that was going on, right? That was my excuse anyway.

The confidence that I'd had when I'd said we needed to talk was gone, and in its place was the Charlotte who just wanted to go home, sit on the couch, and eat chips. Or maybe ice cream. Ok, I'd go home and eat whatever I could get my hands on, and if it meant crossing food groups, I was ok with that.

Hoping he'd changed his mind too, I waited. Eventually he closed his mouth, and his expression shifted as he looked at me. "Mm, no, we're still talking. Let's go."

And proving that he already knew me well, he plucked the keys from the ignition and got out of the car, leaving me no option but to follow behind him.

Awesome!

TEN MINUTES LATER...

Things I'd rather be doing than drying off while I waited to have the conversation with Levi Townsend.

1. Plucking the hair out of my legs with tweezers, one by one.
2. Condition each strand of my hair individually.
3. Getting the Declaration of Independence tattooed over my back.
4. Learning how to crochet.
5. Learning how to crochet plucked leg hair into blankets for fairies.
6. Walking through snake-infested water trying to find fairies.
7. Giving someone an enema.
8. Cleaning out an infected wound with a fairy sized swab.

"Swear to God, Charlotte, if you don't come out and sit down, I'm coming in there," Levi called through the closed door of the bathroom, pulling me away from my listing.

Throwing down the towel, I pulled on the sweater he'd passed me when we'd gotten through the door, seeing as how we were both drenched from the five second run from the car to the house.

I expected him to be sitting down and waiting for me, so when I came face to face with his chest, I jumped and an embarrassing squeak came out.

Pressing a hand to my chest, I tipped my head back to glare up at him. "Must you do that?"

He knew what I meant. He had a habit of appearing – yes, appearing – when I least expected it. I'd even looked up those kids shoes that squeak when you take a step, but they didn't come in 'big ass, hairy man feet' size.

Rolling his eyes, he bent over and pressed his shoulder into my stomach, then lifted back up again with me now over it.

"Let's go," he muttered, walking us down the hallway and back through to the living room.

Some women might have been offended by this, but not me. Straightening my body as much as I could with my arms out wide, I started singing the chorus of the Foo Fighter's *Learn To Fly*. When life gives you lemons, you have to make the most of it.

I was just heading into one of the verses when he bent down and gently dropped me on the couch, and then stood back up with his hands on his hips.

"You're such a dork."

Yes, yes I was, but that had been fun. That's not to say that I wasn't still nervous and anxious, but when you get the chance to do something like that why not take it? What do you really have to lose? I'd spent years being suffocated by my parents, not even making decisions about my own life, so enjoying my freedom was a big deal. If that enjoyment came in the form of me being a dork and singing, why the hell not. Not that he'd said the words as an insult considering that his lips were twitching, and if I could carry him he'd probably do something similar.

That's why I shrugged, not taking even a little bit of offense at what he'd said. "Yup, I am, but if you ever decide to do that again, just to say – I'm totally onboard with it."

For the first time in what felt like months even though it had only been days, he laughed in front of me, the deep husky noise making goose bumps pop up on my arms. "I'll make sure I carry you as often as I can."

We'd had a lighthearted friendship since day one, and I hated how tense I'd felt around him on the way here, so these words lifted the elephant-sized weight off my shoulders. I could take a lot in life, but not having the easy that I had naturally with Levi? No.

"Will you also help me tape the weird handle thing in my car back on before I go home?"

The smile dropped from his face, and this time he glared down at me. "Hell no, I will not do that," he growled, leaning down. "I'll do you a big favor, though, and take it to the junkyard to be scrapped. It's a fucking death trap, and you know it."

He's right, I did know that, but still. "I need that car, it's how I get to work. I don't quite think that getting those shoes with wheels in the soles would get me there quickly and safely, do you?" Although, it had to be said that I'd always wanted a pair.

"I'll give you my old truck," he suggested, moving to sit down next to me on the couch. "I only kept it for emergencies, so it's not like I'll miss it."

"Unless there's an emergency," I pointed out.

Shifting so that he was now facing me with one leg on the couch pressed against mine, he rubbed a hand over his beard. "We've got work ones that I can use if there's an emergency and I need a different vehicle, so that's a moot point."

"You might think so, but it kind of isn't. Plus, your trucks are up here," I held my hand as high over my head as I could, "and I'm all the way down here. I'd need to take a running jump to get into it." I wasn't exaggerating either.

Thinking it over, and more than likely remembering me struggling with his truck, he just shrugged. "We'll figure it out. I'll give you a ride home tonight and take you to work in the morning, and we'll get the vehicle situation sorted out tomorrow."

Groaning, I let my head drop back. "I'm not taking your truck, and you're not taking my car." When he didn't automatically agree, I decided changing the subject was the safest thing to do. "So, what did you want to talk about?" I asked, raising my head back up to look at him, seeing him looking off to the side.

Looking back at me, he just nodded his head slowly. "It's time."

"Time for what?"

"I want to know why you're doing your bucket list and living like each day is your last one. I want to know why you can't relax when we're walking around the store. I want to know why you jump whenever your phone rings. I want to know why you won't talk about your family. And I want you to open your eyes and realize that this isn't your last breath or your last day, and to let me in."

Shit!

I wanted to go back to the conversation about the vehicles now, but with how determined he looked, there wasn't a chance in hell that I was getting out of this without telling him the story.

Damn it, Charlotte, why did you have to go and ask such a stupid question.

CHAPTER FIVE

Levi

I hadn't meant for it to come out like that, but I can't say that I regretted it now.

We'd been tiptoeing around this for months, and if she thought I hadn't picked up on what I'd just asked her, she was wrong. I saw everything she did and noticed every time she thought of something that upset her. I knew her likes and dislikes, what made her tick, and I also knew that she had a lot going on inside her brain that would most likely suffocate her if she didn't let it out. I wanted to take some of that burden for her, shoulder it so that she didn't have to struggle under its weight.

I wanted her to let me in.

All I could do now, though, was pray that she wanted to let me in. So, I sat there holding my breath and waited, not looking away from her. I watched as what I'd said sank in, and I watched as she more than likely weighed up the pros and cons of telling me. Patience wasn't something I was known for, but I drew on every ounce that I had.

Finally, she reached her decision. I'd imagined a lot of possible scenarios when I'd thought about what could be going on in her life, but what she told me... I doubt anyone would have imagined that.

TEN MINUTES LATER...

"So, your dad had an affair with a young receptionist, and you were the result?" I clarified, pacing back and forth in front of her.

"Apparently."

"And you're like a genius, or something?"

Shifting on the couch, she pulled her knees up in front of her, resting her head on top of them as she watched me. "No, I'm not. I was educated at a fast pace and had to work my ass off."

Stopping to look at her, I asked a question about something that hadn't been covered during her story, almost choking the words out. "Did they abuse you?"

Shaking her head slowly, she looked up at me sadly. "No, it was never like that, but they ignored me. If I disappointed them, they acted like I didn't exist, totally cutting me out of conversations and not even asking the chef to set a place for me at the table."

I wasn't an expert on definitions and all the things that could constitute abuse, but that seemed to count to me. "I'm so sorry, Lottie." I meant it to sound empathetic, but it came out croaky and weak.

Who the hell does that to their child? After what happened to Luna, I wasn't blind to the level of asshole parents could get to. She'd been physically abused her whole life unless her brother Madix was around. And now Charlotte... what the fuck was wrong with people?

"I like that," she whispered. Seeing my confusion, she explained, "Lottie. No one's ever given me a name like that."

Moving over to sit next to her on the couch, I tried to be ok just being near her, but it wasn't enough. Reaching over, I lifted her up and placed her on my lap, needing to hold her and understanding why my brothers did this with their wives.

"From this moment, your life is changing. I don't give a shit about all the hocus pocus that woman told you was going to happen. *I'm* going to make sure that nothing ever touches you again, and that only good shit happens."

Her response was whispered softly, but I heard it and the sad tone she said it all in, regardless. "You can't promise that, Levi, no one can."

Watch me – I was a Townsend. Think what you want, but we were the most tenacious family out. When we set our minds to something, we did it... well, within reason. Obviously my childhood dreams of becoming an Olympian athlete hadn't amounted to much, but something like this? Yeah, I could make that happen.

First, I needed to make sure I had the full story straight. You can't help to fix things for people if you don't know how deeply they're broken, right? "So, they were basically paying people off?"

"That's what they said."

"And your boyfriend and best friend were fucking each other?" It was a crude way to put it, but come the hell on – he'd been snorting drugs off her. Call me old-fashioned, but that wasn't what I'd class as 'love making'.

"Yup, after he'd tried to get me to do stuff in the library, I guess he needed an outlet," she snickered, not sounding all that upset about it which confused me.

What he'd tried to get her to do pissed me off and grossed me out at the same time. He had to know she was innocent and not the type of person who'd do something like that. Then a thought occurred to me. "Do you think your parents were paying them off, too?"

Fiddling with the hem of the sweatshirt I'd given her, she took her time answering. "I don't know for sure, but part of me thinks they might have been. They both come from families that aren't hurting financially, but money talks, right? Even if they had money from their parents, I doubt they'd have said no if mine offered to pay them, too."

"And drug habits are expensive," I pointed out, wondering if that's why he'd behaved like he had in the library. "Do any of them ever get in touch?"

"I haven't heard from Amber since I got here, but Eric still sends me emails to my old email address. I changed my phone number and email when I got here so they don't have those, but the last time I checked the old one there were about ten from him."

"And what does he say in them?"

"I don't know, I don't really read them," she shrugged, sounding tired.

Like I said – in all of my musings about what her story might be, not once had I thought anything like this. Did it mean that I'd changed my mind? No, I was more determined now to make sure she knew her real value, but I also realized I needed to take things slowly with her, too. It was easy for me to make a decision and act on it, but she needed to feel secure and get the shit out of her head that the hokey pokey chick had told her about her future.

I knew she trusted me as well, but after what her friends and family had done to her, I also needed to make sure that it was a deep trust and that she knew I'd never hurt her. I'd rather wax my beard off than do that.

Things were going to change, and I knew just how to do it.

"So, this bucket list... what have you always wanted to do," I asked, and then added, "that you didn't find online?"

Living life to the max was the best way to live it if you asked me, but finding things to do from online searches wasn't the way forward. Sure, it gave you ideas, and you got to have fun, but life should be full of all the things *you* want to do, not what someone else had decided to do.

Charlotte tilted her head back to look at me and thought it over. "I've always wanted to ride a horse."

Well, that wasn't a problem – and I knew just the horse.

Two days later...

"This is Night Rider," I introduced Lottie to Archer's horse, wondering if I'd done the right thing when I saw how much bigger than her he was.

Maybe we had a donkey? My cousin Cole had one of those tiny horse – would that be better for her?

Slowly reaching up, she touched his cheek with the tip of her finger, her whole body freezing when he twitched. "He's beautiful. Why did you name him after the TV show?"

Leaning against the side of his stall, I watched as Archer brought through the saddle and shit they needed. "It's night as in the time of day when it gets dark," he explained, brushing down the horse's back.

Seeing how closely she was watching what he was doing, I suggested, "Why don't you teach Lottie what to do, Archer?"

"I'd love that," she whispered, smiling when Night Rider nudged her shoulder with his nose.

My brother was the quietest out of all of us, the one who thought more than he spoke, and who appeared hard but was really a gooey mess inside with females. So it didn't surprise me when he held out the brush to her and said, "I think he likes that idea. Let me lead him out of the stall to that open spot over there, and we'll get him saddled."

I stood to the side watching as they brushed his back and Archer explained about the importance of making sure that there was nothing in his hair to irritate his back with the saddle on it, and then took her through the different stages of putting the saddle on a horse.

Once it was done, he moved next to me as she led Night Rider around getting used to how he walked, and letting him get used to her, too. I didn't know that 'bonding time' was a thing with horses but it made sense, and if it kept her from being thrown off, maybe they should spend a month doing it.

When she was further away from us, I leaned over and whispered, "Do you think he's too big for her? Maybe I should get Cole's tiny pony?"

"He's almost seventeen hands," he replied, crossing his arms in front of him. "That makes him just above average. How tall is Charlotte?"

"About a foot shorter than me, give or take an inch." It was definitely taking an inch, seeing as how she was five-feet-two inches tall, but hey.

"She'll be fine."

Just then Night Rider stopped and shook out his mane, letting out what sounded like an angry grunt at the same time that made me freak the hell out - internally, where I didn't look like a dick doing it.

When he didn't rear up or run off with her trailing behind him, I let out a breath. "Jesus."

"You know," he mused, "if you'd taken an interest in horses, you wouldn't be shitting your pants right now."

Yeah, because that would make it better. "She's a tiny little speck standing next to an equine beast," I hissed. "If that was Bonnie, you'd be doing the exact same thing."

Shooting me a glare, he looked back at what was going on. "I think she's ready to ride him now."

And for the next two hours, I lamented the fact that I hadn't brought a change of boxers with me. I also chewed down my thumbnail to the point that it was bleeding. I may even have considered the merits of those little flasks of whisky people sometimes carry in their pockets. I loved to watch her smiling as she bounced on the saddle, but every muscle in my body was frozen, ready to run if she looked like she was going to fall.

Then there was the way her tits bounced each time... it was a small distraction that made me uncomfortable in my pants, and I had to make numerous adjustments because of it.

The moment Archer taught her to trot and then told her to speed up slightly as they rode around the ring next to the stables, was hell – pure hell. Each bounce… the way her hips moved, her tits shuddered, it was like the weirdest form of porn ever.

And just when I thought I was going to have to take a five-minute break, far away from where they were, Archer called out the words that solved my problem.

"Ok, I think you're done for today. Next week we'll take him out on the fields and really let him run."

The fuck you say!

Charlotte

I loved riding, I loved Night Rider, and I loved that Levi had set this up for me today. I'd expected him to look at me like I was crazy when I'd told him I wanted to try it, but instead he'd made it happen.

There was only one thing I didn't like – the pain. I didn't realize it when I was in the saddle, but riding a horse causes a lot of pain when you get off again.

The insides of my legs felt like they were bruised, my boobs felt like they'd taken a beating, and every muscle was screaming at me for help. And we had to walk back across the fields to where Levi's truck was parked. It hadn't seemed that far when we'd walked to the stables from his house, but the walk back seemed like it was miles away. Just thinking about it made my mind and vagina whimper, and every step almost ended up with those whimpers being audible ones.

True to his word, he'd replaced his truck for my old banger the night he'd said he was going to, even though he'd been sneaky about it.

He'd driven me home that night saying that with the weather it was safer that in his truck, and the next morning his 'old' truck was parked in the space at my apartment, and the keys had been put in my mailbox.

Initially I was pissed, but when he explained that he'd taken a quick look at it and the vehicle had actually definitely been a death trap, that feeling had faded slightly. Apparently my tires were bald, the engine was overheating, the wiring had something going on with it too which was why the little warning lights were always on, the exhaust had holes in it, there was rust eating through the floor under the brake pedal... it literally was a death trap like he'd said. I also didn't have the money to get it fixed or buy a new one, so until I did, I was stuck driving his old truck.

This now left me with the herculean task of getting into the vehicle every day, though. Or at least it should have. The first day I'd had it, Levi had picked me up from work and told me that one of the guys he knew was attaching some sort of step on it, and that he'd get it back to me later.

I had every reason to be dubious about how nice he was being, but here's something I'd realized the first time I'd met the Townsend family – they were genuine people. Sure, they were crazy and they had their faults, but deep down they were just amazing people who cared. I'd had moments where I'd thought they were too good to be true, but the more time I spent around them, the more I realized the truth about them.

And this left me with a conundrum. I was planning for the 'what if', the worst scenario possible because of that damned reading. Could I have a relationship with someone? Would he even want one with me, or was it just friendship?

And I also had my second bucket list notebook full of sexual things that I wanted to try, had no experience at all, and Levi had a penis – one that I'd taken quick looks at through his pants from time to time. I couldn't help it, it just happened.

This left me in a predicament, because I wasn't sure what I could do. The thought of any other guy touching me or helping me work through the second bucket list made me gag, but Levi? Hell yes. Not today, though, and not with how bruised my poor vagina felt after taking a pounding from the saddle.

"Swear to God," I groaned, widening my legs slightly. "I feel like I've been hit in the crotch by a rhino. Why does it hurt so much?"

Snorting, Levi slowed down, then threw his arm around me and gently pulled me into his side. "I've only gone horseback riding a couple of times, but I remember it feeling like that, too. Those saddles are torture on the bone ranger," he chuckled as he gestured at his crotch. I could only imagine what bouncing in the saddle did to a guy's dick and balls. "We'll run you a bath when we get back and throw some Epsom salts in."

Maybe if I wasn't in so much pain, I wouldn't have asked what I did next. "Will that fix my vagina?"

Bursting out laughing, he went to reply, but a voice calling out our names stopped him. "Hey, you guys! Whatcha been doi... Holy shit, are you ok, Charlotte?"

Looking up, I watched as Ariana made her way toward us. Whereas I'd been waddling and walking like a penguin, she almost glided as she walked. Lucky bitch!

"Just took Lottie riding on Night Rider," Levi told her, raising his voice slightly to cover the distance still between us all. "She's feeling the aftereffects."

When she reached us, she made a sympathetic face. "I remember that feeling. It's like you've had a hundred kicks to the cooch, and every muscle in your body is trying to break free."

"Something like that," I mumbled, ignoring the snickering coming from Levi.

"You got Epsom salts or those muscle soaking things y'all had when we were kids?"

"Just headed to do that now," he nodded, and then swept me up off my feet. "I'm going to carry her the rest of the way."

I wanted to argue, but it really did hurt. So, instead I buried my face in his chest and offered up a token, "I can walk, it's ok really." Which was a lie. A big, fat rhino horn to the cooter sized lie.

I wasn't a wimp, and I had a good pain tolerance, but Jesus Christ, this was pushing the limits. Plus, I got to snuggle into Levi for a couple of minutes, and he smelled good – not like a horse and bruised vagina like I did.

Moving so that his mouth was next to my ear, he whispered, "Little liar."

Every hair on my body stood up, and a little shiver made its way through me just from him doing that one little thing. Swear to God, if my vagina wasn't the mess that it was, I would have had an orgasm from that one little action from him. He could say whatever he wanted from now on, so long as he did it like that. It was that awesome.

Regardless of the state I was in, the second bucket list was now looking more important than anything. When I got home, I was going to do an internet search on how to seduce a man - there had to be ideas and tricks online - and I was going to use all of them.

Well, I was going to look up how to cure vaginal bruising from horseback riding first, though. There was no way I could do anything when it was like this, and Archer said we were going out into the fields with Night Rider next week.

I had to fix it and seduce him before I got back in the saddle, because if this was what it felt like after just a trot, I was going to be out of commission for months after a proper ride.

CHAPTER SIX

Levi

I couldn't focus on work or sit still. Two days ago I'd had Lottie in my house and naked in my bath. Naked, as in no clothes at all, and I'd been on the other side of the damned door. I couldn't even count the amount of times I'd asked her if she was ok or if she needed anything, really hoping she'd say yes and I'd get to go in. Getting a 'no' back each time had been frustrating as hell, and I still couldn't get rid of the tension from it. And trust me, I'd tried everything.

And just thinking about it now was making me shift in the chair in my office, and I had to reach down to adjust myself because my poor dick felt like it was being strangled. It sucked. I swear I had more control over my body than this, hell I'd even jacked off in the shower this morning, but nothing was working.

Just as I was getting up to go and try walking it off, there was a knock on the door and the cure to my problems opened it – my best friend Luna, along with her daughter Jamie who was sitting on her hip smiling at me.

"Hey, Uncle Levi," Luna called out, closing the door behind her. "We just thought we'd come in and say hi to you."

My problem solved, I reached out for my niece. "Hey, mama. Hey, precious girl."

Passing her over, Luna snickered when Jamie leaned forward and gave me a slobbery kiss on the cheek and rubbed her nose in my beard. I loved when she did that unless she had those runny booger things kids got – that shit just wasn't cute.

The first time it'd happened, I'd almost said fuck the beard and ripped it all out. I like to think I'd matured since then, though, and I always made sure I checked the kids' faces before I held them now.

"Thank you for my loves, Jamie," I chuckled, grinning down at her. "And I'm definitely happy to see my two favorite girls."

"Oh, the lies," Luna sighed dramatically. "We both know who your favorite is now. She sometimes wears scrubs, has blonde hair... goes by the name of Charlotte."

Leaning against my desk, I tilted my head when Jamie buried her face back in my beard. "Well, it had to happen at some point, and technically you ditched me as your numero uno first."

"He's nicer to me," she shrugged. "In fact, just this morning he..."

"Finish that sentence, and I'll never speak to you again," I growled, glaring at her. See what I mean? My problem from seconds ago was totally cured. Hopefully not for life, though, but it definitely wasn't an issue now.

Shooting me a wicked grin and a wink, Luna leaned back and crossed her legs. "So, how are things going with the beautiful Charlotte?"

Sighing, I adjusted Jamie, realizing that she was almost asleep in my beard, and moved around the desk to sit back down. I was always afraid I was going to drop one them when I was standing up as it was, and when I was sitting down I could lay her out on my lap so she could sleep properly.

"I want more, Luna."

Tilting her head, she frowned at me. "More?"

Looking out the window, I thought about how to describe it properly, but the only thing that came to me was, "I want her. I love being with her..."

"Unless you're jumping out of planes," she interrupted, understanding perfectly how terrifying that was seeing as how Noah had done the same to her.

"Yeah," I muttered, not wanting to relive that moment. "But I love being with her. When I'm away from her, I'm thinking about her. When I'm with her, I want to be closer to her. I'm turning into a freaking middle school girl."

"Don't be dramatic or sexist," she snapped, shaking her head. "Men get feelings like that too, so it's totally normal. So, do you just want her, or do you want something deeper than that?"

I knew what she was asking – was it sex, or did I want a relationship. It wasn't even hard to answer that question. "I want everything with her."

"So what's holding you back?"

I had to think about how much I could tell her without being the dick that told everyone someone else's business. "She's been hurt by family and shit like that. And there was this chick who did some of that card reading stuff on her, and she told her that her life would change when she hit twenty-one."

Looking up at Luna, I expected her to roll her eyes at that, but instead she nodded at me to continue. "So she's made a bucket list of stuff to do in case it means she's going to die or lose a limb, and I've been helping her through it. We've done a lot together, and we've just become close?"

When we'd first started hanging out, she'd told me she had a bucket list and I'd thought why the hell not, it'll be fun. It also meant I got to hang out with her, so I was all for it. Through tattoos, pie-eating contests, ear piercing, jumping out of planes, horseback riding, petting llamas, and shit like that, the attraction I'd felt for her had grown. Now I wanted everything with her.

"*Close*?" she asked. "You want more because you've '*become close*'?"

Wincing, I tried to find the words to explain it, ones that didn't sound asinine and weak. "I thought that we'd just be friends who did things and had fun," I started, and then shook my head. "No, that was a lie. The first time I saw her when Lily was in hospital, I saw someone different to every other woman. I can't explain it, and I don't know why, but there was something about her. Every time I was at the hospital seeing Lily and Rebel, I'd look around for Charlotte, and we hung out and became friends."

"She was great to Lily and Rebel," Luna said softly. "In fact, she was great with Tate and the rest of the family, too."

And she had been. If it hadn't been for her, I think my brother would have torn the hospital apart when we'd first gotten there. "She's got a huge heart, and I hate that no one has ever given her theirs."

"So you pity her?" Luna asked, and I immediately became defensive.

"No, I don't fucking pity her. I want her to experience being appreciated, I want her to know what it's like to be loved by people, I want her to have an easy life where she can do shit and laugh."

Smiling, Luna winked at me. "Gotcha. I knew it wasn't pity, but the only way you're going to be able to figure it out is if you're made to think about exactly what you want with her. If she's been hurt, she needs to know all of this so she can trust you and be herself. She won't truly let go until she knows all of that, Levi, so you need to have it ready to tell her, and then show her."

Fuck it, she was a smart one.

Groaning, I pinched the bridge of my nose with the hand that wasn't supporting the baby who was fast asleep and oblivious to the struggles of her uncle. I missed being a baby, life was so easy back then. "I really like her, Luna, and I want to be with her. She's perfect."

"No one's perfect, Levi," she pointed out.

Looking her straight in the eyes, I said seriously, "She is, just like Noah's perfect for you."

And that was the crux of it. Everyone apparently has that someone out there waiting for them, right? That's what all the romance books and movies worked on – the yin to your yang. She had that with my brother so she knew that feeling, the one where you felt complete around the person.

At this moment, I couldn't know for sure if that was one hundred percent the case with me and Lottie, but I had a strong feeling that it was.

"Then you need a plan to get your woman, my friend," she said simply. "And I'm going to help you."

"We need to do it slowly," I warned, not wanting to jump in there and scare the hell out of the poor woman.

Crossing her arms in front of her, Luna raised an eyebrow as she glared at me. "Her story sounds similar to mine, so I kind of know what she's feeling when it comes to trusting people. If she didn't already trust you, she wouldn't be spending time with you, would she?" She had a point. "You wouldn't know what you know about her, because she wouldn't have trusted you to tell you, would she?" Again, another good point. "So, I'd say the door is there, you just have to work on getting the key into the lock."

Covering Jamie's ear with my hand, I hissed, "We're not discussing my sex life. What my key does in her lock isn't up for discussion."

"I wasn't talking about that, you dirty bastard," she whispered, leaning forward slightly. "It was a metaphor for the last level of trust. Get your mind out of the damn gutter."

Standing up, she walked over to the dry erase board on my wall, and started writing on it. In theory, having a plan was a good thing, but in practice? I just hoped I didn't fuck it up.

Charlotte

It had been two days since my horse riding experience, and I was almost back to normal. Well, as normal as you can be when you're exhausted.

I still wasn't sleeping, so I'd picked up some Melatonin to try tonight. Apparently it 'eased' you into a natural sleep and helped your body get back into a sleeping pattern. I wasn't sure how much of a pattern I actually had considering my job was days for one shift then nights for the next, but I was willing to give it a whirl.

I was at the stage of being so tired now that I was freezing and couldn't get warm. It was November so yeah it was cold out, but normally I was better at it than this. I came from a much colder city than Gonzales, but this winter was kicking my ass.

Taking a shower, I picked up my t-shirt, shorts, and the thick high thigh socks I normally wore during the winter to bed.

I was a creature of habit – anything constrictive while I was sleeping woke me up. I'd seen an ad online for one of those weighted blankets but even thinking about being held down like that while I was sleeping made my anxiety peak. It might work for some, but I liked freedom when I was sleeping. I couldn't even have a feather duvet because they were too heavy for me. Instead, I had a microfiber one with a brushed cotton cover on it that I could kick my leg out of, move around freely under, and that moved when I did.

The need for freedom while I slept meant that I normally slept in shorts, and for some reason the thigh high socks didn't affect me, but they sure as heck kept my feet and legs warm.

Wandering through to the kitchen, I picked up the hot water bottle I'd bought on my way home. The cute pink unicorn cover on it had been what first got my attention, and when I'd realized what it was and that it would keep me warm, well it was a must buy. I wasn't an impulsive shopper - I didn't have the money to be able to do that - but this hadn't been expensive and it would keep me warm, so I'd snapped it up.

And now I was going to fill it up, take the recommended dose of Melatonin, and hopefully sleep through the night.

Once I boiled the water and poured it in without burning myself, then screwed the lid on, I picked it all up and walked back to my bedroom, frowning when I felt a blast of cold air. Taking a look over my shoulder, I made sure that the door to my apartment was closed and that none of the windows were open, and then headed for my bedroom again.

Being tired does strange things to people. Some get angry, some hallucinate, some struggle to stabilize their body temperature, it was different for each person. And the fact that I hadn't slept properly in weeks now, that was worrying me a lot. I couldn't afford to go into work and fuck up someone's life, or have an accident while I was driving Levi's tank, so I needed to sort my shit out, switch my brain off, and get some damn sleep.

Crawling under the duvet, I curled up around my new favorite thing in the world – Princess Sparkle Tits, the unicorn hot water bottle from heaven – and reached out for the two pills I'd left beside the bed along with the glass of water to take them with.

Slowly but surely, I started to fall asleep, and for once my brain stayed quiet.

I WAS LYING ON A SOFT FEATHER THE SIZE OF A BED, WATCHING THE rainbows playing tag. The sun was warm and made my skin tingle, and I was in heaven.

Opening my eyes, I watched the blue unicorn walk toward me, smiling when it sneezed glitter.

"Bless you."

Tilting its head, it stopped and stared back at me. "Charlotte," it whispered, walking over to where I was still lying down. "Open your eyes, you bitch."

I thought they'd be nicer than that. Just then, one of the rainbows dropped and wrapped around my neck, giving me a rainbow hug. It was squeezing, and squeezing, and…

Gasping, I woke up, trying to get some air into my lungs and failing. That damn rainbow was still there, wrapped around my neck. I'd had some strange dreams in my time, but this was the weirdest and most realistic one ever.

"Listen, you bitch," a voice hissed next to my ear, scaring the shit out of me and waking me up fully. "I'll let your breathe if you promise not to scream."

How the fuck was I meant to do that? I couldn't even breathe let alone make a promise, and it felt like I was about to have a heart attack my heart was beating that fast.

Just then, the light beside the bed was flicked on, and through the dancing spots in my vision I saw Eric – freaking cheating, snorting, fuck face Eric Retter – glaring down at me.

The way he was squeezing my throat meant I was getting a tiny bit of oxygen in but not enough, nowhere near enough.

Lifting up a knife I recognized from my kitchen, he turned it from side to side. "I'll only use this if you make a noise."

Then suddenly his hand was gone, and I was able to take a gulp of air and another one. Rolling onto my side, I did my best to get off the bed, but the shock, the fear, and the oxygen deprivation all worked against me meaning that I had no co-ordination and didn't get far.

"Calm the fuck down, Charlotte," he snapped, reaching over and grabbing my ankle, using it to pull me back toward him. "We need to talk."

I wasn't exactly sure I agreed with that statement, especially not after what he'd just done and the knife that I figured was still in his hand, if not close by.

Still, I turned over to look up at him, doing my best to be as still as possible. Irate people made bad choices, bad choices included knives, knives killed people... I needed to keep him calm.

I almost cried with the pain when I swallowed, but I managed to just let out a whimper. "Why are you here?" I croaked, giving in and reaching up to hold my throat. Fuck me that hurt.

Looking genuinely perplexed by the question, he repeated, "Why am I here? *Why?*" Throwing his arms up in the air with the knife still in one hand, he roared, "You left me. I was doing great, I had it all, and then you fucking left. Do you know what I have now, Charlotte?"

There was no way to answer that question, because the truth was – I obviously hadn't even known him. At least, not the real him. I would never have imagined him doing what he'd just done, or snorting drugs off Amber, or even waving a knife around.

Still, I went with a suggestion. "Amber?"

Sneering at me, he began pacing back and forth and I took the opportunity to sit up at the edge of the bed. I couldn't jump up and run if I was lying down, could I?

"Don't be obtuse, Charlotte. I'm talking about the deal I had with Raquel and Ed. The money, the respect. Then you had to fucking ruin it, and now I don't have anything."

I thought I'd been hurt when I'd heard my parents talking. I'd even considered the possibility that Eric had been paid off by them, too, and had almost convinced myself that they had. But hearing it being confirmed? It opened up a raw wound and poured acid and salt in it.

Sliding slowly up to the top of the bed next to where my phone was charging, I waited for him to start talking again and grabbed it off the table, hiding it under the pillow before he saw what I was doing.

Unlocking it with my thumb, I aimed for the bottom left corner to open up my calls and hit the screen. It could only really be one of a few people – Levi, Lily, Tate, Ariana, or Dahlia. They were the only people that I spoke to outside of texting.

Pulling my hand back out, I listened to what Eric was saying now. "...now I've got nothing, Charlotte. Your parents were going to get me a job at the hospital with them and pull some strings so their clients used me. My parents won't give me money, they say I'm a liability and a waste of space. The only thing I ever did that made them happy was dating you."

Crossing my hands in my lap, I tried to look as relaxed as possible when he turned back to face me. "So, why did you break into my apartment, Eric?" I rasped, only just stopping myself from reaching back up to my throat again.

Looking at me like I was the crazy one, he frantically rubbed at his nose, sniffing as he did it. "I'm taking you back with me. If I've got you, then they've got to get me that job, and I can get rid of my parents. Do you know what it's like to be invisible to your own mom and dad?" he shouted, scratching his arms now.

"I do."

"No, you don't. You don't know what it's like to not exist to them and never be good enough for them."

"Yes, I do," I assured him softly, but he was in full on rant mode now, so he probably didn't hear it.

"Always being told you're not good enough, how someone else's kid is better than you. And when you do what they want, you're not doing it properly. Then your mom offered me the deal, and I pictured their faces when I told them I'd got that job and telling them to shove their congratulations up their asses." When he looked up at me this time, I got a good look at how glassy his eyes were.

Still he continued, filling me in on every bad thing that had happened to him from his conception to now.

I watched him more than I listened, taking in how pale he looked, how greasy his hair looked, and how dirty his designer clothes were. He'd always been immaculate before, making sure he didn't have a hair out of place, so I wondered where he'd been sleeping and living.

When his hand movements started to become more agitated and his twitching was becoming more of a full-on body jerk, I focused on his words. "Apparently I was too strung out to be a good doctor, but it was only a little pick me up." He was as delusional as he was high, this guy was coked up to the gills. "Said I'd be a liability. If I went in above the mighty Doctor Retter, he'd…"

Just then there was a loud hammering at my front door that made both of us jump at the same time, and him drop the knife.

"Charlotte," Levi roared, banging even louder on the door.

Spinning back to face me, Eric snarled, "Who's that?"

"My neighbor," I lied. "He's super into protecting the community."

On the next knock, another voice joined his. "Police, open up!" Madix called, almost making me groan. Why did he have to go with the police of all things?

"Police?" he hissed, taking a step toward me.

"I told you, my neighbor has a thing about protecting the

community. He probably saw my light on and wondered if I was sick."

As he went to grab me a loud bang filled the apartment, followed by what I assumed was parts of my door hitting the floor. It was cheaply made so it wouldn't surprise me.

With a hissed, "This isn't over," Eric shot past me, and jumped out the window onto the fire escape, just as Levi, his brothers, and Madix ran into my bedroom.

I want to say I was brave, but I'd be lying. Bursting into tears, I winced every time a loud, hacking sob came out of me and tore my throat into more pieces.

I could still hear the men moving around me, some of them going out the window as well, but a pair of strong arms wrapped around me and pulled me into a firm chest. Maybe I should have been scared, but I recognized those arms and I knew they'd keep me safe.

CHAPTER SEVEN

Levi

It seemed like my family was always in hospital. No matter what we did, we always ended up back here. Maybe we should have family reunions in a hospital somewhere? Then again, we kind of did, so maybe I shouldn't jinx it in case we spent Thanksgiving in the waiting room while one of my brothers had a ball removed from their big toe or something.

After we'd gotten here, the two deputies who'd turned up to the apartment had come to take our statements. Barron and Connor were both good guys and had gone to school with Archer, but I'd been close to losing my shit by the time we were done. How many times did we have to repeat what we knew?

They were going to speak to Charlotte tomorrow, but it looked like she'd just have to write hers out seeing as how she couldn't talk thanks to the fuckhead.

There were currently three members of the PD out searching

for Eric Retter, and if Lottie wasn't lying in a hospital bed right now, I'd be out looking for him myself.

Everyone has a trigger, something that flicks a switch inside them and brings out a dark side. Abuse was mine – especially to women and kids. It'd started with Luna and had grown since then. Now with Charlotte, I wanted to gut the bastard.

To make matters worse, Parker was dealing with a patient who'd been the 'victim' of their car hitting a tree earlier - thanks to the help of the bottle of cheap whisky they'd found in his passenger seat - so we had a doctor I didn't know treating Charlotte.

The guy had immediately pissed me off with his blasé attitude over what had happened to Lottie, and he was taking his time which was pissing me off even more. Did it really take thirty-five minutes to make a call? I could've given him my cell to save him thirty of those minutes.

And now we were waiting again, fucking awesome.

Pacing around the room while we waited for him to review the x-rays they'd taken of Charlotte's neck as a precaution, I replayed what had happened tonight. I was a light sleeper, so when my phone had started ringing with Lottie's tone, I'd woken up and answered it straight away. I'd known as soon as I heard the guy talking that she was in trouble and had contacted my brothers for backup. Madix was a former policeman but the guy still looked scary as hell, so we pulled him in with us. Probably just as well considering his feet were huge and had taken the door down with one kick.

"Will you stop pacing," Luna snapped as she walked into the room with a cup full of ice chips for Lottie. "You're not going to make things go faster doing it, so settle down."

Running my hands through my hair in frustration, I looked

down at Lottie and frowned when I saw her looking up at me in amusement. "What did I do?"

"Don't use your voice," Luna warned her, repeating what the doctor had advised before he left to go to Disney World, where apparently Charlotte's x-rays were. I mean, it wasn't like they were still in the building because it wouldn't have taken him ten fucking hours to look at them if they were.

Looking even more amused at my tiny best friend trying to be strict, she pointed at my crotch. *Nice!* When I just raised an eyebrow, she pointed again and then quickly looked down and back up.

"Baby, I've got brothers who are big old assholes. If you think they didn't pull this trick on me when I was a kid, you're wrong."

Rolling her eyes, she just shrugged and then stared at my crotch instead. Ok, that was a new one. Thankfully, in all of my years of sibling torture, I can hand on heart say that none of my brothers had stared at my dick as a joke, and it was really unsettling.

"Oh, for shit's sake, Levi. Your fly's undone," Luna sighed, shaking her head. "I noticed it when I came in, but seeing as how I don't wanna see your junk, I ignored it and made sure I didn't look down. Poor Charlotte here does want to see your junk," she told me, and I watched as Lottie turned bright red, "so she noticed it, but decided to be nice and tell you about it."

Looking down I noticed that it was true, my fly was undone and that the jockey shorts with *Dude* written across them in neon yellow were very visible. Then again, they were a joke present last Christmas and actually glowed in the dark, so they were visible no matter what, but still.

Before I could do them up, Noah poked his head through the

door. "Dude," he muttered and shook his head. "Any news from the doctors yet?"

Smiling at him, Luna shook the cup at Charlotte to see if she wanted another chip, and then put it down on the table beside her when she shook her head. "Not yet, but it shouldn't be long now," she told him. Turning back to Lottie, she asked, "Have the painkillers helped?"

Here's how badly the fucker had squeezed her neck – she couldn't swallow pills, so they'd given her the option of an injection, a different medication in a liquid form, or a suppository.

I was no expert on the injuries that could result from being strangled – aside from death, obviously – but someone's throat being so bruised that they could hardly swallow? That was bad. Thankfully, she'd gone for the liquid version which meant that she wouldn't have to stick painkillers up her ass when she was allowed to go home. Again, not an expert, but I had to hazard a guess that she'd need help with that, and I couldn't even be around when one of the babies diapers was changed.

Nodding slowly at her, Lottie looked worriedly over at me. It took everything I had in me to relax so that she'd do the same, and then I gave in and sat down next to her on the bed.

"As soon as Doctor Asshole gets back from Disney World with the results of the x-rays, I'm going to spring you from the joint, and you're coming home with me, baby. You'll be safe there," I reassured her, leaning down and kissing her gently. "I'll even get you a little bell so you can ring it when you want anything."

"He makes a good bitch," Noah added from behind me, making me close my eyes in frustration.

"It's true," Luna agreed, getting a glare from me. "What, you do!"

"If it helps," Tate's voice sounded from somewhere in the hallway, "you can get an app, so all you have to do is press it. The noises get really irritating, too."

"Lily downloaded it, didn't she?" Luna snorted.

"Yeah," he sighed. "But I'd be her bitch any day."

Puffing her cheeks out, Lottie made a silent puking motion, making me chuckle. Thankfully, Doctor Asshole returned at that moment. "Well, there's good news, and there's bad news..."

THE GOOD NEWS WAS – THERE WAS NOTHING BROKEN. I didn't know that there was a tiny bone you could break at the front of your throat, but apparently there was.

The bad news was – Charlotte obviously had some bad bruising. They'd even confirmed how bad it was by sticking a lubed camera thing up her nose and taking a look around. This meant that she wasn't allowed to use her voice for seven days, and she had to go back for them to reassess it before she could.

"So, I guess asking you questions is a no go, huh?" I mumbled, desperate to break the silence in the cab of my truck and wincing when I realized I'd asked a question. "Sorry. So, what can we talk about? Not that you can talk obviously, but I guess I can talk at you, right?" Again with the questions.

Sighing, I glanced quickly at her and then looked back out the windscreen at Noah's taillights. "Ok, let me just get this out there now – I'm going to fuck up. I've just asked you two questions in the space of thirty seconds so I think that's more than obvious, but I'm going to look after you and make sure you get better. I'll also keep you safer than you being locked in a panic room, so you don't need to worry about that. I'm not great with medical shit, but I'll do my best. I'm just glad you don't have to put the medication thing up your butt," I rambled, breaking off when I felt her squeeze my arm.

Slowing down slightly, I looked over at her. "Yeah, baby?" Fucking questions, Levi!

"*It's ok*," she mouthed at me, and held up a thumb in case I didn't understand.

Rubbing my hand down my face, I blew out an exhausted breath. "It is ok, and it's not ok, Lottie. He should never have got to you and you shouldn't be sitting there with a throat that's all bruised up. But it'll be ok from now on, I'll make sure of it."

And then she did something that strengthened my resolve even more. She unclipped her seatbelt, almost giving me a heart attack as I slowed down, and scooted across so that she could rest her head on my shoulder and put her arm around my waist. I wasn't that great at reading body language or the female mind, but I assumed this meant that she was showing me she trusted me to protect her, as well as probably trying to comfort me.

Dropping a kiss on the top of her head, I drove us carefully back to the house, avoiding as many of the potholes as possible on the road leading up to it. I couldn't avoid all of them, though, so I wrapped my arm around her and held her as tightly against my side as I could.

"And those damn things are getting fixed tomorrow," I growled, when I pulled to a stop in front of the house.

Picking Lottie out of the cab, I carried her carefully to the steps leading up to my porch. Mom had stayed behind to help watch the babies, but she was waiting for us at my front door.

"Is she ok?" she asked, moving Charlotte's hair away from her face and smiling at her gently.

"Bruised to fuck and back," Noah told her as he walked up behind us. "But the worst thing is, she's got to put up with Levi being her bitch for at least a week."

Standing next to him, Tate added, "We discussed it on the way back, and when she's better we'll choke Levi so that she doesn't have to hear him for at least a week." Leaning around Mom's back, he winked at her, "You're welcome."

Shooting them a glare, I walked past Mom and into my house. I didn't know about anyone else, but I could always tell when she'd been here. I wasn't a messy person by any means, but everything just looked different after a visit from her. The coasters on the table were stacked properly, the cushions on the couch were placed perfectly, there weren't any dishes drying in the kitchen, and if I was right she'd put on a load of laundry.

Turning to look at her, she shrugged. "I wasn't sure if your towels were clean, and you can't have dirty towels with a houseguest."

"I have spares," I pointed out. "A lot of them."

"Well, I didn't know that."

"You got them for me!"

Sighing, she pointed at the nearest couch where there were some pillows and a blanket ready and waiting. "Do you want to put her down here, or does Lottie want to go to bed?"

Looking down at her, a thought occurred to me. "I'm going to put her down while I go and get something for her to change into." She'd been wearing those clothes when the dick attacked her, so there was no way she was wearing them to sleep in.

Doing just that, I went and grabbed a pair of sweats and a hoodie. "She can't wear your sweatpants," Mom gasped, looking horrified. "She's half the size of you."

"I'll go get some of mine," Luna offered. I hadn't seen her come in, but seeing as how Noah was here and she'd been with us at the hospital, it made sense. "Is that ok?" she asked Lottie, who nodded.

"Fine, but she wears my hoodie."

Sitting down beside her on the couch, Mom leaned into Lottie and whispered, "Men. He'll have you carrying a pair of his boxers in your pocket next."

The laughter was silent and it sure as shit looked painful, but after the night she'd had, it was a beautiful sight when Lottie did it.

Charlotte

Staring at the clothing on the couch beside me, a thought occurred to me. I could still feel him on me. It wasn't just that his hands had been on me, but he'd breathed on me, looked at me… I needed to get rid of it. I wasn't panicking or freaking out inside, I just felt dirty.

Looking around, I tried to find a piece of paper and a pen so I could let them know. The doctor had told me not to talk but really that advice had been unnecessary. Every swallow and movement was so painful now that the adrenaline had worn off that I was trying to avoid even moving my head, and the last thing I wanted to do was talk, so there wasn't going to be any arguments from me on that.

A pad with a pen on top of it was placed on my lap, and when I looked up Levi was watching me worriedly.

Picking up the pen, I wrote out: *I need a shower.*

Reading it, he nodded and looked over at where his family were still standing. "She wants to have a shower and then I'm going to put her to bed."

Walking over, Tate patted me on the head and asked him, "Do you need anything done?"

One corner of his mouth lifted in a smile as he watched his brother still patting me gently as I rolled my eyes up at him.

"Yeah, she's got some prescriptions that'll need done. Doctor Asshole gave her some shit to bring home, but I've only got enough for two doses." Reaching into his back pocket, he pulled them out and passed them over to him.

When Tate continued to tap the top of my head, Levi sighed, "Will you stop petting her like a freaking dog, dude. With the way your wife works, she'll change her name to something funky."

With one last pat, Tate took a step back. "I think the odds are in Charlotte's favor, man. It's not like the names can get any worse than what she's already called the animals."

I wasn't exactly certain that was the truth.

Gently helping me up off the couch, Levi turned me around to say goodbye to them all. It was his mom, though, who came to give me a hug.

"Try to get some sleep, honey," Erica whispered, giving me a gentle squeeze. "If you need anything just get Levi to call me, ok?"

God, she was such an amazing woman. Feeling tears building, I pulled back and nodded at her, giving her a small smile. I couldn't fake what I was feeling inside, after everything that happened it just wasn't possible.

Looking up at her son, she warned, "Look after her."

Giving her a hug, he walked her to the door and waved at them all. Once they were gone, he turned to face me looking me over carefully. I'd thrown on a pair of sweats and a bright orange hoodie before we'd left my apartment to go to the hospital earlier, so I wasn't sure it was that great a sight. Not that I had it in me to give many shits right now, but I'd probably have died of embarrassment at any other time if he'd seen me like this.

"Well, at least we'd still be able to see you if you went out in the dark wearing that," he joked, but I could see how forced it was.

Moving over to where he was, I wrapped my arms around his waist and buried my nose in his chest, relaxing when his arms went around my back.

"Tap once if you're ok and twice if you're not," he mumbled into the top of my hair.

That question wasn't easy to answer – it wasn't a case of a clear yes or no. I'd been attacked tonight, strangled and held at knifepoint by a crazy person on drugs. The answer to that part of the question was an obvious no. But now I was safe, and I knew he would do everything to keep me that way. He was supporting the parts of me that had been hurt, and taking away the vulnerability that I was feeling. This meant that in a way, I was ok.

Leaning back, I held up two fingers to him to let him know there were two answers.

Frowning, he asked, "Two? Is that two taps?" Shaking my head, I waited for him to try again. "There are two answers?" he guessed, smiling when I nodded my head.

Holding up one finger, I used my other hand to tap twice,

watching as the smile dropped slowly from his face. Then, holding my finger back up again to show him this was the second answer, I tapped him once and then pointed at him.

Reaching up, he carefully cradled my jaw in his large hands and leaned down to give me a soft kiss. "We're going to work on your second answer being the only one you give when I ask you that question again, I'll make sure of it." I knew he would. "But first, you're going to have a shower and get into bed. You need sleep to heal."

This I knew was the truth, sleep would help me both physically and mentally. Leaning back, he looked down at me and tapped me on the nose, the action so different from his gentleness only seconds before. It worked, though, because I couldn't stop the grin that it brought out, but I sure as shit could stop the giggle that had almost come with it.

Seeing the grin, he winked at me and then picked me up and started walking toward where I assumed his bathroom was. I'd obviously been to his house before so I knew where the guest bathroom was, but I hadn't ventured any further into the place.

When we entered the huge room with slate tiles on the walls, an old-fashioned looking bathtub on one side, and a huge shower on the other, I fell in love. It would be impossible not to. There was a beautiful mix of modern and old, and with the sinks and bathtub being white, the contrasts between it all made each feature stand out.

Placing me down in front of the shower, he stood back and made a frustrated noise. "Ah, shit," he groaned, rubbing his face with his hands. When I just raised my eyebrows, he sighed, "The shower's voice activated."

Well, that was a problem now, wasn't it?

CHAPTER EIGHT

Charlotte

Not for the first time since I'd met him, I felt sorry for Levi. He'd worked out a system for me to shower which involved me knocking on the glass.

To get it to start, he'd yelled at it through the open door of the bathroom. After that, I was to knock once if I wanted it to be warmer, then twice for cooler. When I was done, I knocked three times on the glass and he yelled at it to stop. Admittedly, I thought his shower was freaking awesome – if you had the power of speech on your side, that was.

After I'd gotten dressed, we'd faced a new dilemma – where I would sleep.

He had two other guest rooms, but one was an office and the other one was down the opposite end of the hallway. If I needed help through the night – or what was left of it – it's not like I could shout out, and I had to agree with him when he'd pointed out that there was a possibility I'd have nightmares or flashbacks about what had happened to me. So, with no arguments from me, he decided I'd sleep with him in his room until I felt more comfortable being on my own.

Which led me to now - warm, exhausted, in pain, and unable to switch off. It wasn't what had happened per se that was preventing me from sleeping, but the information Eric had blurted out during his ranting. Even the fact that he'd dated me for money wasn't the problem. I didn't have a high opinion of the guy as it was, so I wasn't surprised now that he'd stoop as low as he had. He'd proven tonight he was willing to stoop a helluva lot lower than that, too, so I guess I was kind of numb to that part of it all.

No, what was bothering me was that my parents had controlled everything in my life to the extent that they had. And I couldn't understand why. If they didn't want me, why had they done it? They obviously had nothing to gain or lose by me even living with them, so why? And I wasn't sure Eric was telling the truth about his own parents either. I'd been around them a lot, and you couldn't hide behavior like that – again, I knew this firsthand from my parents. And, if he was lying, should I call them to warn them about what he'd done?

There was also the fact that I had sweatpants on instead of shorts. I wasn't feeling the way I normally would yet, but I wasn't sure if I'd be able to sleep with them on and I didn't have anything to change into.

"I can hear you thinking," Levi muttered sleepily from behind me, making me smile. His long fingers running through my hair and gently massaging my scalp made me purr inside the safety of my brain. "I would ask if you wanted to talk about it, but…"

Reaching behind me, I pinched the first part of him I hit, blushing when I realized it was his butt cheek. Could have been worse, could have been his penis or a ball, I guess.

Moving closer to me, he wrapped his arm around me and tugged my back into his front. "You know, thinking about it while you're tired won't actually solve anything. You'll create more questions for yourself, get more wound up, and then end up an anxious wreck." Damn those Levi-smarts of his. "Things always seem better after you've had some sleep, and it's easier to clear the fog so you can see the answers."

Nodding my head, I tried to follow his advice, but it wasn't easy to just switch my brain off.

When he realized how much I was still struggling, he sighed and adjusted his position so that his mouth was closer to my ear. "If you ever tell anyone I did this, I'll deny it and make you drink out-of-date milk," he warned, making my eyes shoot open and stare blankly at the dark wall in front of me.

What the hell kind of threat was that? And what was he going to do?

I didn't have to wait long to find out, because he started humming a tune that sounded familiar, and then softly sang Eric Clapton's *Wonderful Tonight*. His deep husky voice crooning the words of possibly one of the most beautiful songs ever written? Out-fucking-standing. I wanted to listen to him singing it on repeat for the rest of my life, but unfortunately sleep won.

I don't know if it was his singing, the fact I felt safe with him, or how exhausted I was, but I didn't even dream.

I JERKED AWAKE, HEARING THE SOUND OF THE SHOWER running from the adjoining bathroom. I didn't even need to swallow to know how much worse my throat felt than it had last night. The only way to describe it was like a python trying to strangle me while a porcupine did the Charleston inside – fucking ow!

"Water off," Levi's deep voice ordered, making me smile.

I had no idea there were voice activated showers nowadays, but I guess it made sense. I wonder what would happen if you answered a call during it and said the word cool? The amount of fun you could have while someone was in there, tampering with the temperature was insane… unless you were the one in there. Which made me wonder how many times one of the brothers had done that to Levi. I'd be too paranoid to use that shower if I was him.

The bed dipped behind me and a droplet of water landed on my cheek, making me wrinkle my nose. "Morning, baby," he said softly, moving my hair off my neck and groaning. "Shit, that looks bad. Tate's gone to fill your prescriptions, but I've got the shit the doctor gave us last night. I'll go get it for you."

Know what's weird? People having a conversation at you rather than with you. I didn't even have to shake or nod my head, he just acted like I had. It wasn't irritating – although I was sure at some point it would be – it was just strange.

Getting up, I sat with my back against the headboard, wincing at the new aches and pains in my body. Apparently sleeping had brought them all out, even in the areas I didn't know would hurt. My neck and head were no surprise, but I actually ached all the way down to my hips, most likely from where I'd tensed my muscles trying to get away from him or trying to breathe. Basically, I feel like shit - I think that about sums it up.

Hearing Levi walking back down the hallway, I slowly turned my head, stopping at roughly the two inch mark. After that, it was a case of moving my shoulders instead, and doing it at a pace that would make a snail look like *Speedy Gonzales*.

Walking in, he noticed how stiffly I was moving and frowned. "That bad?"

Did he actually expect me to answer that question?

Leaning over, he passed me a syringe with whatever the doctor gave us last night in it. I should have been more aware of what was going on at the time, but Luna had been telling me what she went through with her father, so I'd been slightly distracted. Her story was far, far worse than mine, but I got the feeling she was making sure I knew I wasn't alone.

Swallowing it carefully, I leaned back against the headboard and frowned. What was I meant to do with my time? From education to work, I'd never sat down idly. I didn't have any hobbies, I didn't really even have any interests. Hell, I think that much was obvious by the fact that I couldn't even come up with my own bucket list items and had to rely on internet searches for ideas. When I looked at it like that, the state my life was in was kind of depressing.

"Tate's going to stop by your apartment and make sure that your door's fixed and secured properly. He's also going to pick some stuff up for you," Levi told me, sitting down carefully beside me. "Is there anything specific you want him to pick up for you?"

Looking at him out of the corner of my eye, I raised my thumb. Grinning at me, he picked up the pad and pen that I hadn't seen him drop on the bed, and passed them to me.

"Make a list, Lottie, and tell him where to find the stuff, too."

My list consisted of the normal stuff.

- *Underwear (sorry)*
- *Socks (including the big balls of black and gray ones)*
- *Clothes (go for sensible, warm, jeans, t-shirts, sweaters etc.)*

- *Black coat from hanger next to door*
- *Shoes (Uggs and sneakers)*
- *Toiletries from bathroom (I don't have a lot, so throw it all in the bag)*
- *Makeup bag from bathroom - again, there isn't a lot so just throw it all in*
- *Flat irons for hair - not clothes in case you were confused*
- *Hair dryer*
- *Purse next to door - brown one*
- *Phone charger - plugged into next to bed with the pink cable*
- *Laptop*

And then I remembered something and bit my lip trying to figure out how to word it so that he wouldn't be tempted to look inside it. My normal bucket list notebook was in my purse so that was ok, but my naughty one was still under my pillow.

So I added:

- *I left the notebook with my college work in it on my bed. With everything that happened it might be under my pillow. Could you bring it for me so I can get some work done, please?*

That ought to do it, and it was unlikely that Tate would know that I didn't still do actual college work. Studying for my CNRN wasn't the same, although I guess I could do that while I was off, too.

Passing the pad back to Levi, I watched him take a photo and send it to his brother, smiling as he read what was on it.

"Is there really work in that notebook?" I nodded, looking as innocent as possible. "Uh huh, I'm calling bullshit."

He could call whoever he wanted, I was going to hide that book as soon as it got here. If it wasn't for the fact that I didn't want to risk anyone else coming across it – you never knew who was going to go into an apartment that was technically a crime scene, even if there wasn't any evidence to find in it – I'd have left it where it was.

Shrugging, I gingerly scooted across to the bed, lowering my legs carefully to the floor.

Helping me to my feet, Levi held me against his chest. "Do you want to leave having a shower until he brings your stuff back?"

I had no underwear to put on and these were Luna's sweats, so that was a resounding yes. Nodding, I pointed at my teeth. I desperately wanted to brush them and just freshen up a bit. I don't know if it was because I wasn't talking or using my mouth, but my teeth felt freaking gross.

"I've got a toothbrush set out next to the sink with toothpaste on it for you," he assured me, hitting the nail on the head first time. Turning me to toward the bathroom, he patted me on the ass and gave me a nudge. "Go brush your teeth and I'll get you a cup of coffee."

Making my way there, I waited until I heard him leave the room. Here's where I had another issue – going to the bathroom while he was around. I wasn't exactly comfortable with him hearing me pee and I don't even want to think about what was going to happen when I needed to poop.

So, as soon as I knew the road was clear, I sat down and tried to do it so that it didn't hit the water directly and make that telltale sound. I should have maybe just turned the faucet on, but I'd remember to do that next time.

Finishing up in record time, I flushed and washed my hands, then looked down at the toothbrush waiting for me, smiling when I saw he had in fact put toothpaste on it like he'd said.

Avoiding looking at my throat in the mirror while I brushed my teeth, I thought of whatever I could to distract myself. It was Thanksgiving next week, and I'd already been planning to spend it with the Townsends after they'd insisted I join them. How would I manage being surrounded by them and not be able to talk? And the food, how was that going to work? Hopefully, I wouldn't have to puree my turkey because that would just be awkward and gross. I'd never tried baby food, and the thought was disgusting so I'd have to do my best to get to the point where I could at least swallow small mouthfuls by then.

Rinsing off my toothbrush, I placed it in the holder next to Levi's and dried off my face. Taking a deep breath, I made sure everything was tidy, before walking back out into his room where he was now sitting on the edge of the bed with the biggest mug I'd ever seen in my life in his hand. How much coffee did it hold? And where the hell did you get a mug that big?

Looking down at it, he shot me a smile. "It was a gag gift," he snickered, turning it around and showing me a picture of a rooster on the side with **Big Cock** written under it.

The laugh that came out of me sounded like a frog being run over, and it hurt like a bitch, but there was just no avoiding it.

Holding my throat with one hand, I went to wipe under my eyes with the other one, but a rough thumb got there first.

"Sorry," Levi murmured, looking worried as he wiped under the other eye. "Probably shouldn't have made you laugh."

Sighing, I went and picked up the pad.

I'm not an invalid, and laughing is good for you. I'm not going to break so stop worrying, it's just a sore throat.

"Just a sore throat?" he asked incredulously. "Have you seen your throat? It looks like you were attacked by a psychopath."

I was! I wrote down and then passed it to him.

Sighing, he passed the pad back to me and stared at the wall for a moment. "Noah's got tickets to a football game on Saturday. It's for charity so I don't know who's playing, but do you want to go with me?"

Pursing my lips, I pretended to think it over. I'd never been to a football game – no shocker there – so hell yes I did. Looking up at him, I gave him a grin and let him see how excited I was about it.

I didn't even know what happened in a football game apart from them throwing and kicking an egg-shaped ball through a big H, but I definitely wanted to go.

Pulling me into his side, he chuckled, "We'll take you through the rules first so you know what to expect. But it'll be fun, I promise."

Turns out, I should have said no. Not that anything truly bad happened, just something that would embarrass me for the rest of my life.

THREE DAYS LATER...

"Now remember," Levi said as we took our seats. "No yelling out, no screaming, and no cheering. Got me?"

Nodding, I looked around us at the rows of people in different color shirts, some holding up big foam hands, and most holding food of some form. Sigh, I missed food. Everything I ate just now was mushy and like baby food. What I wouldn't give for some popcorn.

Turning back, I noticed we were two rows away from where the field was. I maybe should have realized that when we first sat down, but the atmosphere here was infectious, so I was distracted by what was going on when we'd taken our seats.

I really did want to scream and cheer, even though I didn't have a clue what I'd be doing it for but still. I also wanted to raise a huge foam hand up in the air and yell... and I definitely wanted one of those tubs of popcorn that a majority of the supporters seemed to be holding.

Just then, a big foam hand appeared in front of me and conked me on the nose. "Here you go," Lily snickered, holding up her own. "We figured you'd enjoy one of these. The next time Levi asks you a question, you can just hold it up and he'll see you even from the other side of the room."

Grinning at Levi, I looked back just as she shoved a huge mouthful of popcorn in her mouth. I'd never even been a big fan of the stuff, but now I want it badly. I wouldn't mind the bits that got stuck in your gums that you then have to spend ages brushing out, or the little piece that wedged itself between two of your teeth and you have to perform surgery with dental floss to fix – basically, all the parts of popcorn that deterred me from eating it before now weren't an issue at that moment. I was hangry, and I wanted to get popcorn wasted.

"No," Levi rumbled, somehow reading my thoughts through the back of my head.

Sighing, I leaned back in my seat and fiddled with the big foam hand. He didn't need to remind me, trust me I could still feel the pain. The swelling and bruising to my trachea hurt like a mother, and as much as I wanted the popcorn and to get popcorn wasted, it just wouldn't be worth it. Even the huge plastic cup he passed me filled me with trepidation. Anything carbonated would make it hurt, anything too cold would make it hurt, anything acidic would make it hurt... I was like one of those assholes who made the waiter go back and forth ten times to get his drink right in a restaurant. I'd always hated those guys, so becoming one of them made my ass twitchy.

"Relax, I got them to put a bottle of water in it that hadn't been refrigerated," he winked, taking a big draw on his straw. Lucky bastard.

Within minutes, the players were out and there was a lot of posturing going on. They were hugging, smacking each other on the back, hitting shoulders... and then it all started. There was a coin toss and some of the people watching seemed to be happy with who'd won it, but I couldn't figure it out so I just nodded my head. I didn't want to look like *that* chick – the one who'd just come along to be with the hot guy. I mean, granted that was part of it, but the other part was to experience the game.

And that's when it got interesting on the field. All the players bent over facing each other like a group of Sumo wrestlers wearing helmets and padding, and then I swear to God – one of them bent over and stuck his ass in the guy's face behind him. Glancing over at Levi with my eyes wide, I pointed with my massive hand at it like *what the fuck?*

Bursting out laughing, he pulled me so that my back was against my seat again. "It's meant to happen, dork."

What the hell does he do next, fondle the dude's balls? Although, just to say, if that's what happened I was totally ok with that. I wasn't expecting it, but it would definitely be memorable, that's for sure.

Lily stuck her hand in front of me, recording what was going on. "It's a charity game," she yelled over the roaring of the crowd around us. "I'm recording parts of it for the charity to put on their website." Skimming over the crowd, I could see at least forty journalists and numerous professional cameras trained on what was going on. Pointing them out to her, she

95

leaned in as everyone roared. "Yeah, but they want a spectator's point of view, so I said I'd do it for them."

Fair enough. Settling back, I watched as the game played out. Players running this way and back that way, knocking other ones down, kicking the ball, running like their lives depended on it (although, with the size of the dude behind him, I can't say I blamed one particular guy). And each time they crossed a line or kicked the egg through the H, a buzzer went and people went wild. I might not have understood the finer points of the game, but I was enjoying the hell out of it. In fact, when I got home, I was going to look up the different teams and pick one to follow.

Still watching, I picked up my big ass cup and was about to take a mouthful of my drink, but – and as embarrassing as it is to admit it – I sucked at sucking right now. Sucking through a straw hurt my throat because of the pulling and tightening of my throat muscles. Fuck it, even in my head that sounds filthy, but there was no other way to phrase it.

Feeling my cheeks burning, I pulled the lid off and placed it on my knee, ignoring the look that Levi was giving me.

Apparently he wasn't too good at reading signals and body language, though. "I would give a thousand dollars to know what was making your cheeks that color."

No, trust me, you wouldn't.

Just as I was raising it up to take a mouthful of water, I lowered it and reached for some of the napkins that Lily had placed between us when she'd sat down. Apparently, it wasn't unusual for things to spill at games – especially when things got rowdy and arms were flying around – so she'd come prepared. Seeing as how the rim of the cup was wide, it would be just my luck that I'd take a mouthful and tip it down myself.

Holding the napkins under my chin this time, and mentally patting myself on the back for being so conscientious and protecting myself from potential embarrassment, I tipped the cup up and opened my mouth just as something happened on the field and everyone jumped up and started screaming around me.

Almost like it was happening in slow motion, Lily's arm swung out knocking the cup in my hand, and shooting some of the contents onto Levi's crotch as he stood up cheering with everyone else.

Looking down and seeing the spreading wet patch over his dick, he growled, "What the hell?"

And this, folks, *this* is why we have voices – to talk our way out of situations like this. To apologize like nice people do, blame it on the twat beside them who was still jumping up and down, totally oblivious to what had happened. Not that Lily was a twat, it had been an accident and all that, so she was just a little bit of one.

Reaching over and grabbing the whole stack of napkins, I yanked Levi back down into his seat and started furiously rubbing at it. People were going to think he'd peed his pants, and he'd never talk to me again so I had to fix this.

Chuckling awkwardly, he tapped me on the shoulder. "Whoa, Lottie, it's ok. It'll dry."

Yeah, that it would, but I was just so freaking embarrassed by it all that I just wanted to make it disappear. If anyone saw it, he'd never live it down. And there were cameras out there, what if a photo ended up online?

Through all the rubbing and worrying, I didn't notice that the stadium had gone quiet around us. Nothing registered except drying off that fucking wet patch. Why did shit like this have to happen to me? Why couldn't I have been the person who did moves like they did in the *Matrix*, and duck in slow motion when Lily had bumped into me?

"Uh, Charlotte," Lily hissed, poking me in the side. "You might want to stop…"

"*Ladies and gentlemen,*" a voice boomed through a speaker. "*Let me remind you that there are children at this event, so if we could keep ourselves in check and not let the excitement carry us away…*"

Confused, I picked my head up and looked behind me at Lily who was pointing her phone at something high up on the field now.

Following where she was looking, I saw that I was on one of the huge screens which had previously showed the scores and video replays. Now it had me, bent over with my head in Levi's crotch as I rubbed at the…

Oh, fucking bird shit on a feather, no!

And that's when I discovered the best use of the huge foam hand and placed it over my face. I was aware of Lily curled up in a ball in her chair, laughing her ass off, and a high-pitched squeaking wheeze coming out of Tate, but aside from that I was now in hiding for the rest of my life. And Levi Townsend and his poor molested cock totally didn't exist in hiding.

The one time I got taken out to do something fun, I ended up spilling water on Levi's dick, and then got video footage of me trying to dry it played across the stadium from an angle that looked like I was jerking the poor guy off.

Once I got over the embarrassment of it, I was going to look online to see if that had ever happened to someone else – there was totally comfort in numbers in this scenario. That's if I survived the embarrassment, and the jury was out on that one right now.

The shuddering coming from Levi became hard to ignore, but I was going to do it. Well, until he tugged me under his arm and pressed his face into my neck, making my body shake as he continued laughing.

"I'm so sorry, Lottie," he snickered, not making me feel better at all. "But you've got to admit – after what happened a couple of days ago, that was the funniest shit ever."

He had a point, but it wasn't him who'd molested a nice guy's penis. If he'd done it, he wouldn't be laughing.

Tugging the foam hand away from my face, he used his thumb to turn my face toward him. "Baby," he whispered, choking halfway through the word – the big rat bastard. "Look at me." Reluctantly, I did what he asked, and was surprised by the soft expression on his face as he looked at me. Running the tip of his nose down my own, he mumbled, "Thank you for being you. You've given me more laughter in the short time I've known you than anyone, and I can't imagine my life without you in it."

Whoa. It was cheesy as hell, but shit I loved it at the same time. And it meant a lot to me to hear it, especially after the stadium had witnessed me violating his poor crotch.

Grinning at him, I decided to live for the day. Hell, I'd already jerked the poor guy off with water and napkins on a huge television screen, so what could I possibly have to lose?

And on that thought, I leaned in and kissed him, making the first move for the first time in my life, and hoping I wasn't fucking up even more.

CHAPTER NINE

Levi

"She's already embarrassed enough, so don't make it worse," I warned my brothers, making sure they knew how serious I was.

Thanks to the fucking internet, clips of Charlotte trying to dry my crotch had gone viral. Thankfully, my family had kept her distracted with Thanksgiving prep so she had no idea they existed and had been seen by thousands of people – yet. It was only a matter of time, though, given how often she looked shit up. I'd never known anyone to do as many internet searches as she did. Wouldn't you run out of questions or shit to think up?

Looking slightly offended, Noah sat up straighter in his chair. "I wouldn't do that to her, none of us would."

"Not intentionally, no," I agreed. "But our family has a habit of joking around about things, and I'm worried that this will make her withdraw. Don't forget, she's never had this in her life, so she's not used to it."

"Neither was Luna," Noah pointed out quietly. "At least, not until you brought her home with you that first time."

Tate was uncharacteristically quiet throughout all of this. Archer, Madix and Rich were in the room, too, but they weren't the ones I was worried about the most. Although Archer and Rich had an uncanny ability to piss off Dahlia's best friend Bonnie and Lily's best friend Beau, they tended to be more reserved and gentle with the other female members of the family.

Speaking of which.

"Has anyone seen Ariana recently?"

My sister had been spending more time away from us all since Parker moved to Gonzales County, and it was starting to worry me.

"Saw her at the bar with Bonnie and Beau last night," Rich replied, the muscle in the side of his jaw ticking at the mention of the woman who we all knew drove him insane.

I wasn't sure what the back story was between them, but there was definitely something there, something juicy. I had enough of my own shit to worry about, though, without digging into his.

Hearing Bonnie's name, Archer straightened out of his slouch. "Why didn't you call me?"

Flicking him an annoyed glance, Rich muttered, "I wasn't aware I had to."

"Well now you are."

Watching them closely, Noah crossed his arms in front of him. "What the hell is going on with you guys? You obviously like them, why not just make shit right?"

Rich had worked with us for years and was like a member of the family, so no offense was taken when he shot Noah a dirty look. "And how exactly do you propose we go about doing that, oh wise one?"

"Apologize," he replied simply, raising an eyebrow. "You know what that is, right? The word sorry, flowers, chocolates, maybe a few pecks on her ass cheeks."

"And is Parker meant to do the same thing to Ariana?" he challenged back.

This was where I needed the topic to change. She was my baby sister and the thought of her and a guy made me feel like stabbing myself in the brain with an ice pick. We'd all known she had feelings for the guy since my cousin Tom's wife was kidnapped and we'd gone to help find her – maybe even before that seeing as how he'd always been around when we'd gone to visit them all – but feelings and actions are very different things.

For months she hadn't been ok, changing from her normal happy self to someone who looked like she had a ten ton weight on her shoulders. Then he'd moved to obviously be closer to her, and she'd distanced herself even more. I didn't like seeing my little sister hurting, and even though I was preoccupied with what was going on with Lottie just now, I didn't like that she was distancing herself from us. That shit better fix itself soon.

Finally, Tate broke his silence. "Not to add more shit to your already overflowing plate, but does anyone know if our grandparents are coming to celebrate with us?"

It's funny how one question can make your colon turn inside out, whilst at the same time make the three quiet members of the group laugh theirs inside out, too, isn't it?

FIVE HOURS LATER...

Walking tiredly through the house, I made my way toward the bedroom, not noticing Lottie curled up on the couch. It had been five days since she'd been attacked, and thankfully she hadn't shown any psychological aftereffects from it.

She'd written down that it was because she was safe, she felt safe, and she knew that it was an isolated event. She'd also said that as scary as it had been, she didn't feel like he'd hurt her – although I begged to differ on that one – and that she wasn't going to let some drugged up, small pricked, asshole ruin her life. Again, I begged to differ on that, but I was relieved she was strong enough mentally and emotionally to not let him continue to affect her.

It wasn't that I thought he'd ruined her life, but he'd definitely hurt her and scared the shit out of her. I really was proud of her for being strong, but I didn't want her to feel like she *had* to be strong because I was going to do that for her. She'd shouldered everything from the day she was born, it was time she let someone else do it for her – me.

As I passed the couch, something moving on it made me jump until I saw she'd been sitting writing in her notebook while she waited for me. She still couldn't talk and swallowing food was still painful, so it wasn't like she could have called out my name, so I should have been more aware.

Changing direction, I walked over and squatted down on the floor in front of her.

"Hey, baby." The smile she gave me every time I called her that was worth every eye roll and gag my brothers made when they heard it. Some of them were hypocrites, the other one would find out when he finally got the woman he wanted. "Sorry, I had to get some paperwork finished and I was talking to the guys. Have you had a good night?"

The blush that filled her cheeks when I asked that question intrigued me, but then I looked down and saw what she was wearing and almost groaned.

On her second night, she'd come out of the bathroom in a pair of shorts and these thigh high sock things, almost making me inhale my tongue. When I'd asked her if she wanted me to get her a pair of sweats to sleep in – desperate for her to say yes – she'd told me that she struggled to sleep in bulky clothing and wore these during the winter. The night before had apparently been a fluke and was more than likely down to the painkillers and stress of what had happened. This meant I slept next to a wet dream and fell asleep every night hoping I didn't embarrass myself in my sleep.

How could socks be that hot?

Looking down at the roughly four inches of bare flesh between the top of the socks and the bottom of her shorts, I mumbled, "I'm in the deepest, darkest depths of hell."

Unable to help myself, I lowered my forehead onto her thigh and took deep breaths trying to clear my mind. Unfortunately, with where I was, all I succeeded in doing was breathing in her scent with my face inches away from her pussy, which just made it all much worse. Then, just to add to my struggles, her small fingers started to run through the hair on the back of my head, scratching gently with her nails.

When I couldn't take it anymore, I lifted my head up and focused on her face, seeing her confused expression at whatever she saw on mine. Catching her hand, I brought it up to my mouth and pressed a kiss on the palm of it. The line between doing what I figured was the right thing at this moment and doing what I wanted was as thin as a strand of human hair, but my control snapped when I saw her look down at my mouth.

"Lottie, you've got to know that I have feelings for you," I began, pausing when I saw how shocked she looked. *Seriously?* "You didn't know that?"

When she shook her head, it raised a new question for me. Was she that naïve, or was she not as clued into me as I was to her?

Reaching up, I gently cupped the side of her face, avoiding her neck completely. "I do. I've loved the heck out of the time we've spent together, and I know that this isn't exactly great timing to tell you all of this, but I want more with you."

As soon as the words were out, I almost winced. *I want more with you? That's the best you could do, Townsend?*

"I wouldn't ever force you to do anything, and it won't change anything if you don't feel the same way about me, but I need you to know where I'm at."

Her face softened to an expression I hadn't seen before as she raised her hand to skim the tips of her fingers over my beard. Please don't let that expression be pity!

On one hand I wanted her to be able to speak so she could tell me she felt the same way, on the other hand I was glad she couldn't in case she didn't. But the longer we went with just her gently touching my face, the more I started to panic that she was thinking how to let me down in a way that wouldn't ruin our friendship.

Needing to say something, I added, "I wouldn't ever do anything to hurt you, you know that. And…"

Whatever else I was going to say was cut off when she leaned down and kissed me, her hand moving off my face and around the back of my neck like she was trying to stop me from pulling away from her. Letting her lead, I leaned in closer to her, waiting to see what she did next, and shuddering slightly when the tip of her tongue skimmed across my lower lip. Our mouths opened at the same time, and then her tongue was skimming across mine, and I could feel her breath hitting my cheek as she let out little gasps.

Unable to help myself, I trailed my hands up her thighs and wrapped them around her sides to pull her into me, ignoring the pain starting to set in from being on my knees on the ground for so long. That pain faded into the ether when her legs lifted up to wrap around me, holding me tightly against her.

Before it could go even further, I reluctantly pulled my mouth away from hers and waited for her to open her eyes.

When I saw her baby blues looking back at me, I whispered, "I don't want to take this somewhere you're not ready for, Lottie. This isn't just a one-off for me, so there's no need for us to rush into it."

Reaching out, she grabbed up her pad from the couch and started scribbling on it. I could throttle that bastard myself for many reasons, one of them definitely being not being able to hear her voice right now. Passing it over to me, I read her uncharacteristically untidy writing.

I'm fine. If I didn't want this with you, I wouldn't have kissed you. Trust me to know what I can take and to tell you if I can't take it. Please!!!!

The underlined words and amount of exclamation points made her tone obvious, but even more so was the fact that she'd almost torn through the paper with how hard she was pressing down with the pen when she'd written them.

Taking a calming breath in, I passed it back to her. "Ok, but the second you feel like you've hit your limit, I want you to promise that you'll either tap my shoulder or smack me across the head. Can you do that?"

Grinning at me, she nodded her head.

Getting to my feet and wincing when my knees cracked as I straightened them, I leaned down and picked her up. I'd intended on carrying her to the bedroom like that, but she twisted slightly at the last second and wrapped her legs back around my waist.

"You're determined to push my buttons, aren't you?" I murmured, the grin on my face showing how I really felt about it.

This was one of the things I liked about Lottie – she knew her own mind. I didn't want someone who went along with things just to make me happy or for an easy life. I wanted to know what my partner wanted, to look forward to the unknown with them instead of it being dull. I wanted to be challenged by them. Life wasn't easy and I needed a brightness there that made it easier to handle, and Charlotte was that brightness for me.

I'd toed off my boots when I got in like I did every time I came home, so my footsteps were silent as I walked us in the direction of the bedroom. I could feel my heart racing, and I'd be lying if I said my hands wouldn't be shaking if they weren't full of her ass cheeks at that moment.

Almost like she could sense exactly how nervous I was, she leaned it and started gently kissing the side of my neck, almost making me trip when I felt the first brush of her lips.

Here's something that I'm sure romance books and movies don't show – there were downsides to having a beard. I had mine because I hated shaving, I suited the beard, I liked the beard, and it kept me warm in the winter. Simple, right? Well, it was also the current fashion – everyone went on about beards and alphas, and how sexy they were, so the beard definitely caught people's attentions.

What they didn't explain was that beard hair falls out, and at that moment I had a mental image of her getting a strand of it in her mouth and choking or spitting it out. That's one of the not so sexy sides of having a beard, along with food getting stuck in it and people not washing them.

And for the love of fuck, men of the world, beard oil was made for a reason – use it. It's no lie that with great beard came great responsibility, so look after it and it'd look after you.

My worry about her choking on a beard hair went unfounded, though, so that was a huge relief. I brushed my beard, conditioned my beard, and I oiled it so that it was a well looked after beard machine, but I'd still have gotten rid of it for her. With tears, lots of tears.

My knees hitting the bed pulled me out of my inner beard ramblings, and I realized exactly how nervous I was. Sure, I thought about beard stuff every now and then, but to do it when I had Charlotte wrapped around me, her ass filling my hands? It was all out of desperation to not embarrass myself any second. I needed to shake it off before I kissed her again, or this would be a disappointing experience for her.

Gently lowering her down on her back onto the mattress, I braced myself with my hands either side of her, not giving into the need to just kiss her yet.

"I need to tell you something." When she nodded at me and rubbed my forearm, I went with just laying out the truth for her. "I'm nervous about this. I'm scared of doing something wrong, I'm scared of scaring you, I'm scared that I won't notice if you tap me on the shoulder or slap me on the head... but I want you more than I've ever wanted anything in my life."

I hadn't noticed that she was even slightly tense before I started talking, but when I saw her body visibly relax into the duvet under her, I realized I'd said something really right. Ironically, her being relaxed helped me to do the same, and without thinking about it, I bent my arms so that I could kiss her again.

The position we were in wasn't possible to maintain for too long, what with me still basically standing, so I pulled back, only willing to allow a tiny gap between our mouths.

"If you wrap your arms and legs around me, I'll move us further onto the mattress," I whispered, placing a knee onto the bed.

When she did what I'd suggested, I tucked a hand between her back and the mattress, and used it to support her as I carried us further into the bed, settling her up near the pillows. One of the bedside lamps was on so I could see her properly as I moved her hair off her cheek.

"One day I'm going to get you to do an internet search for me, seeing as how you love to do those so much. I'm going to get you to find out exactly what shade of blue your eyes are so that I can paint my office that same color. If we can't find out the shade, we'll go to one of the home improvement stores that mix up the exact shade of paint you want and get it that way. I might even take my truck in and get it done in the same color," I told her, meaning it wholeheartedly.

They weren't just blue, they were a mixture of a light purple and medium blue that changed with what mood she was in. Right now they were darker than normal and the purple tone was deeper, a shade I hadn't seen them in before, but it was my favorite one so far.

"I don't know what's making them the color they are right now, but I think this is the shade I want."

Quietly laughing, she shook her head and rolled her eyes at me. I wanted to hear that laughter badly, but I'd settle for just being able to see it in the position we were in right now.

Reaching down, she tugged on the bottom of my long-sleeved Henley, and started to pull it up toward her. Helping her along, I reached behind my neck and grabbed the collar, giving it a tug, and accidentally dropping it on her face as it cleared my head. Figuring now was as good a time as any to take hers off, too, I started to pull hers upward as I watched her throw mine to the side of the bed.

Patience didn't seem to be something she had an abundance of right now, though, because she pushed my hands out of the way and yanked it over her head, making me freeze as it passed over her still bruised throat. I was about to tell her to be more careful, but the beaming smile she shot me made me reconsider that choice. I didn't want to constantly remind her about it or make her feel self-conscious, so I'd keep my worrying on the inside for now.

Instead, I kissed the smile, giving her my own when I felt her hips jerk against me. Trailing kisses away from her mouth and down her neck, I stopped to flick the tip of my tongue against her pulse, and then began moving again. I didn't want to spend too long on the area, but in the not too distant future I was going to kiss the area of her throat that had been hurt. I'd wanted to do it since I'd seen the bruising, and now that I had the go ahead to kiss her, I was going to finally get to do it. Not tonight, though, definitely not tonight.

You can get a rough idea of how someone's body will look through their clothing, but nothing prepared me for Lottie's and trust me I'd pictured it many times. The tops of her breasts were almost spilling over the top of her bra and there was a deep crevice between the two mounds that were only slightly smaller than a handful. The bra itself was black lace and gorgeous, but I wanted what it was covering too much to look at it for long.

Reaching behind her to undo it, I frowned when I didn't find the hook thingy that was normally on bras and raised my head to look for it.

"How the hell do you undo this thing?" It came out in a tone that contradicted my earlier declaration that we were going to take it slowly, making her laugh quietly.

And then she did something that would more than likely star in every single one of my dreams for the rest of my life. She reached up her hands to the little satin bow nestled between her tits, and with a quick flick of her fingers, the cups separated and fell to the side.

Groaning, I balanced on one arm so that I could raise the other to skim the tip of a finger around the hard rosy nipple on one side.

Looking over at the other one, I leaned down and flicked it with the tip of my tongue and then gently sucked it, smiling lightly when her hips jerked up into my stomach and her fingers moved into my hair. Lifting my head to watch her face, I pinched the other one between my finger and thumb. The way she tipped her head back and opened her mouth was beautiful.

The more I played with them, the more restless she became under me, so I continued kissing my way down her torso, pausing to skim around the outside of her bellybutton with my tongue. My jeans were becoming more uncomfortable, and each time I moved I was becoming more aware of how they were now strangling my dick.

Hoping I wasn't going to freak the shit out of her, I scooted back until I was standing at the base of the bed and slowly undid the button and zipper, almost letting out an audible groan when the pressure was removed from the area. I kept my eyes on her throughout the whole thing, making sure that she was still with me – which, thank fuck, she definitely was.

Bracing her feet on the bed, she raised her pelvis up in the air and slowly pulled her shorts down her legs, kicking them off once they got to her feet.

Shit that was hot.

Lowering my jeans, I pulled them off my feet leaving them in a heap on the ground, and then slowly crawled back up the bed toward her. Once I got to where she was on it, I went back to the position over her that I'd been in before I'd moved.

"I'm almost certain you don't have a lot of experience," I began, watching as the redness on her cheeks got deeper and she gave a small nod. I'd rather have my prostate checked than have this conversation with her right now, but it needed to happen. "Now that I know that for sure, I think it's best if I show you rather than tell you. Am I right?"

The amount of relief on her face is almost comical, but I wouldn't dare laugh at a time like this. Instead, I turned onto my back and pulled her into me for another kiss to help her relax. Her nipples pressing into my chest made me groan slightly, and her fingers responded by spasming where she was holding the side of my face.

I figured by putting her on top, she'd feel more in control of what was going on and that it might relax her – something which I was proven right on when I felt the muscles in her back under my hand start to loosen.

Moving us so that she was now fully on top of me, her crotch pressed against mine, I explored with my hands, loving how soft her skin was. Years of working for the oil company had left me with rough hands, and every time I skimmed them back over an area on her that I'd just touched, I could feel goosebumps breaking out on the surface of her skin.

I was so caught up in my exploration that I didn't immediately notice when she started to grind down against me. The more frustrated she got, though, the more pressure she added on each grind until I felt like I was going to explode. There was still the thin barrier of my boxers and her panties between us, but the sensation was fucking unreal.

Lifting her head up, she looked me in the eyes on her next grind, almost begging me to do something. "Ok, baby, I get you."

With my hands on her hips, I lifted her up until she was straddling my face and looking down at me in almost horror. "You'll change your mind on that when you feel this, I promise."

Not giving her time to overthink it, I pulled her down onto my mouth, using my thumb to move the crotch of her panties to the side before she reached me. Flicking my tongue between her lips, I watched as she reached out and grabbed the top of the headboard with her hand, her eyes never leaving me once. Angling my chin up, I managed to catch her clit between my lips and sucked down on it, making her gasp.

With her now relaxing, I moved the fingers of the hand that was still holding her panties to the side so that I could slip the tip of my middle finger inside her.

Jesus Christ, she was tight.

Slowly and carefully, I moved it in and out of her, adding the tip of my index finger once she was used to it. It didn't take long for her thighs to start shaking, and that's when I reached up with my free hand and pinched her nipple at the same time that I sucked hard, watching as her head fell back and a barely audible moan came out of her as she came and spasmed around my fingers.

As she started to come out of it, she dropped her head back down to look at me, her eyes half-mast and a small smile pulling the corners of her lips up. Moving my hands so that they were around her hips, I lifted her slightly so she was balanced on her knees, and then scooted out from under her until I could stand at the side of the bed.

I don't know if it was my expression or the fact that I was lowering my boxers, but her panties were off and gone by the time I straightened back up again.

"I would make a joke about speed," I huffed out, pulling her by the ankles toward me, "but I have a feeling I'm about to break a record myself."

Sitting down on the edge of the bed, I reached into the drawer and pulled out a condom and tore the package open with my teeth. This was a no-no in case you ripped the rubber, I knew that, but anyone who managed to actually do that was an idiot seeing as how you could clearly feel it inside the wrapper, and it was common sense to go for the edge furthest away. If you didn't have the IQ to figure that out, you should probably refrain from ever having sex or operating any form of machinery, including a calculator. Harsh, but true!

Rolling it down my length, I shifted back slightly and moved her until she was on her knees straddling me again, with my feet still on the ground.

Looking up at her, I saw her staring at my cock with an unreadable expression on her face. Did she still want to do this?

Charlotte

Physically speaking, tab A inserts into slot B, or the round peg went into the round hole. But until this very moment, the only round peg that had been inside *my* round hole, came in the form of a tampon – something which was much, much smaller than Levi's round peg.

Then again, the average vagina was only three to four inches long normally, but could expand by around two hundred percent when aroused, so the statistics were in my favor with this. At least I hoped they were, because right now I wasn't sure Levi's tab would fit in my slot.

Reaching down, I put my hand around it for the first time, smiling when it jumped slightly. There were roughly only two inches between the tip of it and my vagina, but Levi stopped me as I lowered myself until it was just touching me.

"Baby, we don't have to do this if you…"

Looking up, I stared into his eyes as I notched the tip just inside me. Seeing that I wasn't going to change my mind, he nodded and leaned in to suck my bottom lip between his own.

When he pulled back, he didn't move too far away and whispered against my mouth, "We'll stay in this position so that you can control the speed and how much you take, ok?"

Honestly, I would have preferred for him to control that, but at the same time I understood why and it made sense. Plus, enough porn films were made with actors in this position, so it had to be good, right?

Fitting my lips against his, I kissed him as I lowered even more, pausing periodically to adjust to him stretching me. When I was halfway down, I moved my head so that my forehead was resting against his, which meant that when I opened my eyes back up again I was looking down into his green-blue ones.

"Lift yourself back up again until you're at the tip, baby," he whispered, "and then lower back down."

Not looking away once, I followed what he said, and holy shit it was fucking amazing. Not that it wasn't before, but he was now further inside me and the sensation of his cock pushing back inside me was indescribable.

Doing it again, I didn't stop this time until I hit the base of him – which was incidentally at the same time that he hit the base of me.

There were roughly eight thousand nerve endings in the clitoris in comparison to only roughly four thousand in the penis, and I was almost certain at this point that every last one of those nerve endings was screaming their heads off. It made me feel sad for poor Levi's cock who was only feeling half of what I was, but I'd apologize to it later.

As awesome as taking it slowly was, soon enough the need to speed up my movements took over, and that's when I felt a similar burn in my thighs to what I'd felt when I was horseback riding a week ago. Had it only been a week ago? Jesus, it felt like it had been months, but now that I was riding Levi I was even more grateful for the lesson in controlling my thigh muscles. That said, it probably also meant that my legs would be screaming at me tomorrow which would suck because I wasn't sure I ever wanted to stop doing this, and if they did that I'd have to.

I'm not sure how, but Levi obviously read something in my expression and the grip that he had on my hips changed to helping support me as I moved. On the next plunge down, he stopped me from rising back up again and moved my hips forward and backward, making me clench down around him.

Every time I tried to cry out or make a noise, all that would come out was the sound of air, and it was really starting to piss me off. I wanted to scream out or even yell his name – until seconds later when an orgasm hit me out of nowhere, and then I wanted to be the woman screaming that I was coming. Instead, all I could do was open my mouth and try to get enough oxygen into my lungs to survive it. That might not sound like a hardship, but trust me, it was.

Levi held my eyes through every clench and spasm, and never once stopped moving me up and down his length. I wasn't sure how he did it because the last thing I had enough of was the cognitive functions to remember to keep moving.

Just as it started to leave me, he pressed his lips against mine and grunted into my mouth, not closing his eyes once as I felt him pulsing inside me.

Remembering what he'd done while I was coming, I ground down into him and then moved my hips slightly, watching as his eyes widened in surprise at the move. With a shuddering breath, he finally closed his eyes and groaned deeply, holding me tightly against him.

Wrapping my arms around his shoulders, I moved so that my face was buried into the side of his neck.

It had to be said, if this was what Amber's grandmother had meant by life changing at twenty-one, I was going to track her down and give her a bonus. I was also going to enjoy being able to tell Levi 'I told you so'.

If it meant the more sinister possibility, though, well then I had the best incentive for fighting the hell out of it now.

CHAPTER TEN

Charlotte

S hining the torch down my throat, Parker instructed, "Now say ah."

Hiss.

That was it – hiss. Looking over his shoulder at where Levi was watching us with a frown on his face, I raised my eyebrows at him and then rolled my eyes, making his lips twitch. Yeah, it sucked, but it was still kind of funny.

This morning when I'd woken up, I'd felt like I'd done a weeklong trek on Night Rider's back up the side of Everest. The medications that I was still taking to help with the swelling in my throat had been waiting for me and they'd worked on the other aching areas, but it still wasn't a comfortable morning.

That was until Levi ran me a bath with those blessed Epsom Salts of his. I was starting to think that the cure for everything was to add those things to hot water, and if that was the case I was tempted to soak my throat in the stuff. Logically speaking, it would mean being immersed face down in the bath so I'd need a snorkel, but if it meant I could scream Levi's name... I'd snork the hell out of that snorkel.

While I'd been soaking, Parker had called to see if he could come over to look at my throat in an hour, and here we were with me hissing at him. Good times!

Looking down at the screen of his laptop at the x-rays they'd taken when I was in the ER, Parker picked up his phone and looked at something on it.

"You playing Candy Crush, man?" Levi joked, looking nervous.

Wanting to make him smile, I started signing out the only words I knew how to sign.

Hi, my name is Charlotte. I'm your nurse. Can you write down what brought you here today, please?

Sue me, at least I'd started learning it so that I could help more people and keep them in their comfort zones.

Fortunately it worked and he threw his head back as his deep laughter filled the room, making Parker look at him over his shoulder.

Turning back to face me, he raised an eyebrow. "Wanna tell me what that was about?"

So, I did it again, not expecting him to put his phone down and start signing back at me.

Seeing how confused I was by it all, he explained, "I learned sign language so I could speak to all my patients."

I wasn't surprised by that at all, the showoff.

Once he'd stopped laughing, Levi moved over to stand beside Parker, his eyes still shining as he looked down at me. "What's the verdict?"

"Strangulation can cause a number of injuries – the most common being death, which fortunately isn't the case here," he winked at me, making Levi snort. "When they did the x-ray and then looked inside her throat, Dr. Laska diagnosed a high degree of bruising and swelling both inside and out. A hematoma around the trachea can cause problems with swallowing, breathing, and talking, and each patient's recovery is different. Some people's voices are even changed by it forever."

"A hematoma?" Levi asked, sitting down heavily beside me.

"Bruising," Parker clarified, not looking at all surprised and with good reason. Medical terminology was scary, and it wasn't unusual for people to be frightened by that word.

"So, we don't know when Lottie will get her voice back?"

"Unfortunately, no. Health doesn't go by a set rule or play out in a set way, every case really is different. And, even though he didn't press hard enough to starve her brain of oxygen or kill her, he pressed long and hard enough to do substantial soft tissue damage. Even if you were the healthiest person alive, it could take you months to recover from something like that, so it all just depends on what Charlotte's body does from here on out."

Staring at the floor while he thought over what had just been said, Levi hissed, "I could kill that sonofabitch."

"Little tip, press longer and harder around his neck than he did," Parker replied, only just sounding like he was joking.

"And her voice might not sound like it did before?"

Resting his elbows on his knees, Parker focused on both of us. "It could be raspy or a bit deeper," he explained. "But she'd make a killing as one of those sex line operators."

Hearing Levi's sharp intake of breath, I grabbed his hand and gave it a squeeze. When he looked at me, I made the hand movements to indicate making it rain money and grinned.

Before he could say anything, Parker added softly, "She suits you, Levi. I'm happy for you, man."

I liked Parker. He was a great doctor, a good guy, had a kick ass name – Parker Knight - he was a good friend, and he had a huge heart.

I wasn't blind to the fact that he had a thing for Ariana and vice versa, and I didn't know what the problem was that was preventing them from being together. I did know, though, that she hadn't been around recently, but when she was, she was always hyperaware of what Parker was doing, like she couldn't take her eyes off him.

It wasn't up to me to get involved, but I made a mental note to talk to Luna, Dahlia and Lily about it to see if they could help them sort it out.

Ari was tall, curvy, and abso-freakin-lutely stunning. It wasn't those stereotypical type of looks either, more classic and memorable, if that made sense? Stereotypical ones you acknowledged and thought beautiful. Classic ones were unforgettable and packed an extra punch. Parker was also tall, even taller than any of the Townsends, and he was a handsome guy.

He also fit in the Dr. Hottie category, the sexy man with a stethoscope and medical degree. And they both had awesome personalities. Basically, their babies would be adorable, they were suited together, and people would stop and gasp when they saw them together.

And most importantly, they cared about each other, big time.

They just needed to sort their shit out – said the girl who lost her virginity last night at the age of twenty-one.

Levi

Hearing the door shutting behind Parker as he left, I looked at Lottie who was reading something on the screen of her phone.

Sitting down beside her, I leaned into her and started playing with her hair. "What are you looking at?"

It was such a loaded question because she had the most random shit going on in her head.

Shutting the screen down, she shoved it under her thigh and shrugged making me suspicious. At the same time, I was more concerned with how she was coping with the news from Parker. Granted, it wasn't bad news per se, but it wasn't exactly great news at the same time.

"Are you frustrated about your voice?"

Sighing, she nodded and brought her feet up onto the couch in front of her.

I wanted to reassure her in a way that would sound as genuine as possible. "It doesn't bother me, you know, but," I paused, "I do miss your voice."

I'd noticed something over the last couple of days with Lottie – she constantly moved her lips or tried to say at least part of what she was thinking, and that had given me an idea while Parker was examining her.

After last night we definitely had a deeper connection. When you were in a committed relationship with someone, technically sex did add something more to it. Trust, understanding, you started to read their body language, there's obviously a different tension that runs between you both, too, but that wasn't relevant to this. No, I wanted to try to read her lips to see if I could make it easier on her. Maybe it would even add to the bond that was building?

"So, I want to try something, baby. If I can read some of what you're trying to say on your lips, it might make it easier on you. It'd also feel like we were actually talking, in a way."

The expression on her face was unreadable for a moment, but then she nodded at me and waved her hands for me to start.

Here goes.

"When Parker asked you if it still hurts, you said yes. How bad is it?"

This obviously wasn't what she'd expected me to start with, but she answered anyway.

Moving her mouth carefully, she said, "*Yes, it still hurts.*"

Picking up her hand, I pulled her closer to me. "It still hurts, huh? I'll kiss it better later, how's that?"

"*Hell yes.*"

Bursting out laughing, I thought up another question. "What's your favorite color?"

I was expecting her to say pink or blue, something normal like that, but instead she mouthed, "*I don't have one.*"

"You don't have a favorite color?" When she shook her head, I put it in the big pile of things I'd tackle later.

"*Yours is green, right?*"

I wasn't surprised she'd picked up on that given that my bedroom was painted a pale sage green, my bedding was various shades of the color with white sheets, heck even my curtains and the throw cushions on my couch were green.

Laughing, I nodded and added, "I didn't decorate or get any of the stuff for my house. Mom and Ariana did."

Seeing her grinning as she looked around, I suddenly wanted her to feel at home here, too. I got that it was new to both of us, but when the time was right, she was welcome to change whatever she wanted.

"We're not doing too badly at this, are we? I thought it was going to be hard, but so long as we keep it to short answers, I think we've got this." Reaching out, I plucked the secret notebook out from under her thigh and hid my hand behind my back. "I don't think we'll be needing this anymore."

When she shook her head and tried to reach around me to get it back, I deliberately lay down on the couch, sandwiching it between my back and the cushions.

Picking her up, I positioned her so that she was straddling my lap. "What's in the notebook, Lottie?"

Her cringe just made that curiosity worse. "Oh, now you've got to tell me. Is it a diary? Did you write good things about me?"

"A little."

Pretending to be hurt, I gasped, "You wrote that I was little?"

This time when she started laughing, a squeak that was only just audible came out, but it was enough. "Holy shit, you said your first word!"

Lying down on top of me, she pressed her lips against mine and pulled away smiling again. I don't know why, but she suddenly blew out a breath and started carefully mouthing what looked like, *"It's my sex bucket list."*

A million and one – ok, a million and two – possibilities to add to the list hit me just knowing it existed. I wanted to ask if I could go through what she'd written down so far, but I didn't want to push her too fast so I stayed quiet for as long as I could, thinking up things to add to it instead.

Unfortunately, like with most people when they're put on the spot, I was drawing a blank aside from two things: Lottie on her hands and knees in front of me while I gripped a handful of her hair, and her on her knees in the shower with her mouth around me.

Clearing my throat to get her attention and shifting my crotch away from her slightly, I rasped, "I'm suddenly seeing the appeal in internet searches."

More of the little noises came out of her when she laughed, except this time she did it for so long that she ended up holding her throat and wiping away a couple of tears.

Just as she started to settle down, my sister saved her from the other questions I had to ask about her little naughty book wanting to take Lottie out for a drink with the rest of the women tonight.

"We're pausing this conversation here, baby, but it's not over by any means," I warned her as we put our coats on. "I'll be doing my own internet searches, so think about that while you're out with the girls."

CHAPTER ELEVEN

Charlotte

"Ok, if I remove my brother as being the other performer in this equation, I think I can add to your list," Ariana decided, her hand loosely holding her glass of wine now.

It had started off as the women meeting up for 'a drink', and had quickly turned into a merging of souls over the age old bonding by alcohol.

I'd been nervous about drinking anything that would set my throat on fire, especially with noises starting to come out of it, but then someone had suggested Baileys with ice and that was it. It was better than painkillers, better than warm drinks, but definitely not as good as the sex last night had been for it.

Unfortunately, the alcohol had also loosened my tongue – well, my writing hand – and I'd told them about my sex bucket list book. It was now hidden under my side of the mattress of Levi's bed, where I'd put it while he was in the bathroom before we'd left, but we had napkins and a pen so I could just staple them into it.

"Say no to fisting," Luna informed us, holding her fist in the air.

"I feel that goes without saying," Dahlia answered for us all drily, but I was still staring at her fist and picturing the damage it could do.

Making gagging noises, Ariana glared over at her sister-in-law. "You need to find Jesus, Luna. That's disgusting!"

"Seeing as how you've met her and interact with her regularly, I'm uncertain I need to remind you that I've had a child which means that I've given birth," she replied coolly. "Unfortunately, that involves random medical professionals sticking their hands up your cooter to measure how dilated you are. It also involves a child's head coming out of the aforementioned cooter, too. Hence my aversion to and recommendation that fisting be avoided."

This time most of us at the table gagged, except mine was silent. Even as a nurse I couldn't cope with that graphic analogy.

"Never having kids," Ariana gasped, taking a mouthful of her drink.

Hiccupping delicately, Lily held up her hand. "I thought we were meant to be adding things to it, not banning things from it?"

"Maybe we should stop drinking altogether?" Ariana suggested looking slightly green. "It hasn't escaped my attention that three of you here are involved with my brothers, and if I have to hear about y'all's sex lives – or fisting," she glared at Luna. "I'll stab myself in the eye with the umbrella in your drink," she nodded at my glass.

For some reason, Beau had insisted on adding a small metallic pink umbrella to my drinks, and although it was cute, it was inconvenient - well, unless you were Ariana and needed something to stab yourself in the eye with. There was no way to drink out of the glass without it going up your nose or in your eye, so for health and safety's sake, I was making them into a little city beside me on the table.

"Speaking of stabbing yourself in the eye with an umbrella," Luna whispered loudly. "What's going on with you and Parker?"

"He's an ass."

Sighing, Dahlia leaned on the table. "He has a hot ass." And Parker really did.

I worked with the guy so I'd seen him in scrubs on numerous occasions since we'd both started working in the same hospital, and he was the only guy I knew who could fill out the back of those things.

"That doesn't answer the question," Lily persisted. "What's going on between you guys?"

"Nothing, because he's an ass."

Leaning in closely, Luna sniffed the air around Ariana, and sat back. "Y'all kissed. I can smell it on you."

When she just blushed and started fiddling with the corner of her coaster, we knew she'd hit the nail on the head. "So why aren't you together? He likes you, you obviously like him…"

"But remember how he had that chick who was sniffing his dirty gym stuff in those photos," Beau said as she dropped off the next round of drinks, not hanging around for an answer as she walked back behind the bar.

"I hate it when she does that," Lily muttered, picking up a bottle of water from somewhere. "She's got radar ears."

Downing her drink in one, Ariana set the glass back down on the table with a thud. "But she's also got a good point. The chick always had her hair done nicely, she spent time on her makeup, she probably wore heels and sexy underwear, and I'm…" she gestured up and down her body.

I didn't know what the full story was and before she could finish what she was saying, someone walked up beside her and for a second I swear I thought it was the chick we were talking about. The woman who'd joined us was wearing clothing which cost more than I made in six months, her hair looked like she paid thousands for it to be created by fairies every morning, and her makeup was immaculate. And that was just what I could see of her.

"Ari, hey," she greeted, leaning in and kissing her cheek. "How's your brother?"

In all fairness, the question had four possible answers but three of us stiffened when she asked it.

Flicking a glance at me, Ari cleared her throat and shrugged. "He's never been better, Kari. How are you?"

"Good, good," she replied distractedly, looking around the bar. "I've got to go. Tell Levi I'll call him back soon."

Well, I guess we had the answer to the question.

Not wanting to discuss it or cause any awkwardness to what had been one of the funniest nights I'd ever had in my life so far, I picked up the napkin I'd been writing things down on, and started waving it in the air.

Clicking her fingers, Dahlia suggested, "Anal sex, write that down."

It took a second for it to sink through the slight alcohol induced haze in her brain, but when it did, Luna punched her on the arm. "You're married to my damn brother."

"Sucks, doesn't it?" Ariana snickered, enjoying Luna getting a taste of the torture this time.

Leaving them to argue it out, I met Lily's wide eyed look with my own. Leaning in she whispered, "I saw an ad for an anal sex kit if you're going to do that. You get like plugs and lube in it. Although the plugs still looked kinda big," she mumbled as an afterthought.

"How about a threesome?" Ariana suggested, just as the noise in the bar dimmed slightly.

"Now, puddin', you know you're more than enough for me. Why would I want to share you with another woman?" Parker's deep voice asked, making us all jump.

I'll give her credit, even with her cheeks hot enough to fry eggs on and shaking slightly, Ariana responded calmly, "Well, you're not enough of a man for me, so I guess we could ask another one of those to join us, couldn't we?"

I wanted to be her when I grew up. To have that quick wit and be able to answer without her voice shaking, she was like the vixen and wit version of *James Bond*.

I didn't get to hear what Parker said back to her, though, because I was picked out of my chair by familiar hands and then ended up sitting in Levi's lap.

"I think it's pertinent to point out at this point that four of us here are her brothers, and two are as good as brothers," he said over my shoulder, nodding at Madix and Rich who'd also joined us. "Any talk of threesomes or sex between or involving the two of you is punishable by a cactus being shoved up your ass."

Turning her glare onto her brother, Ariana snapped, "Kari's here by the way. She says she'll call you."

Groaning, he leaned his head in between my shoulder blades as Tate asked, "Kari, as in your ex?"

Leaning forward so quickly that I almost face planted in the umbrella city, Levi growled, "Let's get this straightened out before you upset Lottie – and let me make it clear, I will not be happy if that happens. Kari was my girlfriend when I was seven years old. Not yesterday, not a week ago, fifteen years ago, seeing as how I turned twenty-two three weeks ago and every last one of you celebrated it with me. On that very day, she texted me asking me if I could call her about a question she had about renovating an old barn. I said I'd do my best but I didn't have much to do with my house being made, aside from helping the guy draw that shit out. She tried calling me that night but I was celebrating, so I rang her back the next day and she didn't answer. In all honesty, I'd even forgotten that it'd happened."

Everyone stayed quiet for a couple of minutes after it, but always the curious one, Dahlia was the one to break it. "Why did you guys break up?"

Sighing, he nodded at Luna whose eyes had lit up at the question. "Tate told him that chicks had cooties, and if he kissed one he'd end up with tits. He was going to break up with her, but by the time he saw her at recess she was already going out with Danny Brockowicz."

"The guy with the sinus problem?" Ariana asked, wrinkling her nose up. "Gross."

Leaning around my shoulder, Levi pointed out, "It's not like he could help that, the poor bastard had to live with nickname Boogerwicz for years. And I think it was allergies that caused it, not his sinuses."

Just then, the woman herself strolled up to the table, her lips twisting slightly when she saw me sitting on Levi's lap.

Obviously it didn't really mean much to her, though, because she walked around the table until she was behind us, and leaned in to hug him from behind.

"I thought I saw you come in. I've been waiting for you to call me."

Tightening the arm that he had around my waist, he pulled me back against his chest. "I've been busy. Have you met Charlotte?"

Giving me one of those quick to mouth and quicker to floor type of smiles - the ones that disappear as soon as they've happened - she turned back to him gracing him with a genuine smile.

"I really need your help with that barn as soon as possible. The purchase is due for completion next week and I want to get the building started immediately, but I don't know where to start."

"Like I told you, I didn't have much to do with mine aside from deciding on the layout. You should speak to your architect and the team overseeing the renovations."

Beau appeared back at the table with a tray full of drinks for the men and said sweetly, "You should ask Rich for his number, he loves dirty wrecks." Leaving us with no doubt about the amount of shade she was throwing his way.

Catching Lily's eye as she watched her best friend walk back to the bar, I mouthed, *"Awkward."*

Not missing a beat, she whispered back, "No shit."

The feet of Rich's chair screeching across the floor as he stood up from the table made me flinch slightly, but after that I was so caught up watching him walk around the bar and then lifting her over his shoulder, that I didn't even care that Kari was still trying to convince Levi to help her.

Whoa, that was a hot move. Not only did he do that, but he strode out of the bar with her, ignoring her smacking his ass and whatever she was saying to him.

Turning back to face me from where she'd been watching them, too, Ariana fanned herself. "Now *that* was hot. I didn't think Rico Suave had it in him."

"If that's what it takes, baby, I'll throw you over my shoulder right now," Parker told her, his voice a low growl.

Not wanting to show how much he was rattling her, she patted him on the cheek and said sweetly, "And I'll kick you in the balls right now, *baby*." Standing up, she called across the table, "Yo, Kari. Parker here likes high maintenance wrecks, too. He's all yours."

As she finished, she turned to walk away but Parker caught her and pulled her down onto his lap.

"Not interested, Corey," he muttered to Kari, and then started whispering furiously into Ariana's ear.

How had this gone from a drink with the girls to drama central in the space of ten minutes? Admittedly, we'd discussed anal and fisting, but where had all the drama come from?

A tug of my hand got my attention onto Lily who was leaning in so she could whisper something to me. "What you want to do is not make a bucket list of things that are possible to do sexually, but things you really *want* to do. There are different types of sex - some hardcore, some not so hardcore. It all depends on the people involved," she told me, and then paused as she waited for me to digest this sage wisdom. When I nodded, she continued, "Think of all the stuff you think is hot, then put it into action. Have some ass spanking, hair pulling, hot sex with Levi. Then keep having it, and enjoy the hell out of every second."

I doubted that she could have heard what Lily was saying, but Dahlia leaned in and whispered, "There's a book that has four hundred and ten sexual positions. Get overnight shipping on it and get to work." Pulling back she winked at both of us, "You're welcome."

We pulled our phones out at the same time and started typing on the screen. The book actually existed, and it had over a thousand five star reviews, too.

For curiosity's sake I looked at the four one star ones and started laughing when I saw that one of them was from a guy who was upset that a woman didn't come with the book. Another one was from a woman who said she'd injured herself trying position number eleven, and the last two were from reviewers who said their copies had been printed back to front causing a lot of confusion between them and their partners.

With a quick glance at Lily, we both nodded and hit the one-click ordering button.

It wasn't until I was finished that I noticed Levi's movements underneath where I was sitting on him, like I was cutting off the circulation to his legs. As I moved to stand up so that the poor guy wouldn't lose a limb, he caught me around the waist and pulled me closer to him.

Putting his mouth right beside my ear, he rumbled, "Best not to do that right now, baby."

On his next twitch, the real reason for his issue became obvious when his erection pressed against me. I hadn't been aware of Kari leaving us while I'd been looking at the book, or the fact he could see what I was ordering over my shoulder. I'd been so fixated with the book and reviews, it hadn't occurred to me to check what he was doing. I sure as shit knew now, though.

Cheeks flaming, I glanced over my shoulder at him, blushing even harder when he winked at me.

"So why did you guys decide to join us?" Luna asked the men, looking at the various non-alcoholic beverages on the table. "I thought it was going to be just us?"

I felt more than heard Levi's growl, but it was Madix who answered the question. "The man who attacked Charlotte was seen not far from her apartment tonight looking like he was trying to find a way around the back of the building. When the authorities investigated it, though, he disappeared again."

It had to be said: I obviously didn't have a lot of time for Eric after finding him having sex with Amber. Any feelings that could be considered remotely positive – and I was including not giving a shit about the man as being positive – withered after he attacked me. But now, the anger and hatred for him were almost smothering me. And I had my parents to thank for this shit.

This twenty-one shit was a real pain in the ass, but I didn't have the same worries that I had before about it being the year I was killed off.

Now it was a period of growth, and I was counting the days until I turned twenty-two.

CHAPTER TWELVE

Levi

The list of things currently giving me a pain in the ass was longer than Santa's good list. So far, off the top of my head I had:

- Eric and everything associated with him

- Kari

- Rich and Beau

- Archer and Bonnie

- Parker and Ariana

- Not being able to hear Charlotte's voice

- Work

- The adult side of being an adult, i.e. having to act responsibly and not just being able to strangle Eric

- My family

That was a good start, but like the chunk of ice that the Titanic hit, it was only the tip of the iceberg.

When we'd gotten the call about the sighting of Eric, we'd moved quickly to get to where they all were. In all honesty, I think part of it was being hopeful that we'd come across him first and get to deal with him ourselves, but that was more of an unspoken thing.

Then I'd had to put up with various dramas, including Kari, instead of being able to focus on Lottie. It's like someone had put up a notice that the Oscar awards this year were open to the public, so everyone was trying to be the lucky winner.

The most frustrating part was that I could only fix one of the problems tonight, that's all I had the power to do, but I'd definitely done that.

While Lily and Dahlia were whispering to Lottie, I'd taken the opportunity to tell Kari that I knew what she was doing and that there wasn't a chance in hell of it happening. I'd sweetened that with the addition of telling her parents what she got up to last year with someone who was now spending eight years in prison – not that she'd been involved in his crimes, that I was aware of at least. No, Kari had been enjoying the money of the man who'd conned five women out of their savings, and when she'd been questioned over his whereabouts she'd omitted to tell the authorities that he was handcuffed to her bed at that exact moment.

How did I know this? Her former maid was the wife of one of the men who worked for our company and was now employed by my family, after losing her job for telling the police that she'd seen him on the premises one night when she was questioned by them. Apparently Kari hadn't much liked her rich lover being incarcerated and had terminated Fiona's employment.

Somehow, she'd managed to talk her way out of being charged for hiding a criminal, and her parents were none the wiser about the situation. Probably for the best considering her father's position as the CEO of their family owned investment company who boasted some well-known clients.

Putting my list of issues aside – Charlotte had enough problems going on and had been hurt enough in the past. I wasn't going to add to that or let someone who had absolutely no importance in my life do it either. So, easy come, easy go, and that was one thing crossed off the list.

Which led me to now, driving Charlotte home. We'd all decided shortly after she'd completed her online purchase that it was time to go home. I wasn't sure if it was paranoia or fear, but it felt like we were being watched from the second we left the bar, so now I was scanning the road constantly in case something jumped out at us.

Having someone stalk your girlfriend isn't like how it happens in a horror movie. You don't get the scary music, you don't get to see the buildup to the big scene, it's all an unknown. The tension is always there, and it builds up inside you. I can't even count the amount of times I woke up at night to check the house, or jumped out of bed because I thought I'd heard something.

It went without saying that my family weren't strangers to shit like this – which was the understatement of the year – and if there's one thing I learned from all of what we'd been through was that staying stagnant wasn't the answer. Part of what the person wanted was fear, it made them feel powerful and fueled them. It also made you easy to find because you were predictable. No, the key to winning the war was to make it look like they weren't affecting you. Obviously you needed to take the extra measures to ensure your safety, but being unpredictable kept them off balance.

My middle name should have been unpredictable, so I was going to make sure that Lottie was safe, and that Eric had no power over her.

Realizing that I wasn't the only one who was on edge at that moment, I reached for Lottie's hand.

"Lot of drama tonight, huh?" The incredulous look she shot back at me made me chuckle. "The holidays bring out the best in us all. Speaking of which, Mom wanted to make sure you're ok with chocolate pie instead of pumpkin pie on Thursday. We're having pumpkin soup as a starter apparently, and none of us like pumpkin pie anyway."

I wasn't expecting an answer immediately, I was just trying to fill the silence and distract her. I kept talking about the Thanksgiving preparations for the rest of the journey, warning her about the way we celebrated it which made her laugh.

As we drove up toward my house, I realized that we weren't being thrown around like we normally were because the potholes had finally been filled in. I'm not sure how anyone would fail to notice that their brain wasn't being ricocheted around their skull, but that's what had happened when we'd left earlier to get to Charlotte.

I could feel one of those big sneezes building as I stopped the car in front of the house, and sure enough as soon as I cut the engine it came out of me.

Not missing a beat, Lottie passed me a napkin from her purse and mouthed, *"Bless you."*

"Thanks, baby."

Because I didn't need to use the napkin, I was about to drop it in the cup holder when I saw the writing on it and opened it up to see if it was important or if she'd written stuff down that she needed from the store. The things listed on it were clearly not things I could get at the store or ask Mom to pick up.

~~No fisting~~

~~No anal~~ – butt plugs?

Yes hair pulling, spanking, hot sex

See positions in book

Her door slammed shut at the same time as my low groan so she likely had no idea what she'd passed me. She would, though.

Charlotte

Even though I hadn't been working since the incident with Eric, I still had a shower before I went to bed every night out of habit. Needing Levi to yell at his shower for me was slightly inconvenient, but his beat mine by a mile, so I'd waited until he'd yelled it from his bedroom, and hopped in.

I hadn't intended on getting my hair wet tonight, but a pair of strong arms wrapping around me unexpectedly made me jump forward under the spray even though I knew who they belonged to.

Resting his bearded chin on my shoulder, he pulled my back tightly against his stomach, his cock nestling into my butt crack.

"Thank you for the napkin you gave me in the car, baby," he rumbled, plucking the sponge I'd been washing myself with out of my hand. Running it up my arm, he continued, "I agree, my hands are way too big for fisting."

What did he mean about fi… *no*!

His arm held me in place when I tried to spin around to face him, which was probably a good thing because I was fairly certain that I'd chicken out and sprint out of the shower instead. I hadn't wanted to leave the napkin behind for a stranger to find, so I'd thrown it in my purse to bin when we got home. When he'd sneezed, I'd grabbed the first one I could out of my bag, totally forgetting about that one.

Closing my eyes, I prayed for death, anything that would kill me in the next two seconds. If this was what the fortune telling lady meant, I was all for it now.

"Anal would also be a problem for me," he added, running the sponge down the area in question making me gulp. "If you want to try butt plugs, though, I'm sure we can work up to it. Just to warn you, baby, I have issues with the kids even having their diapers changed, so I'm not sure how far into it I'll be able to get. For you, I'm willing to try, though."

To hell with the butt plugs, I wanted to try dying.

Dropping the sponge to the floor, he rinsed me off under the spray and then moved back against me.

"Open your legs wider," he instructed, cupping me between them as I did it. "Anything that you want to try, we'll try. Within reason," he added, reaching up and taking a handful of my hair, then gently pulling my head back. "You want to have hair pulling sex, I'm onboard with that. You want me to spank you, I'll spank you. But I won't ever hurt you, so if I say enough, it's enough and I won't do it harder."

It was hard to nod when my head was as far back as it was, but I still did it knowing that he'd feel the slight movement with his hand holding my hair.

Tilting his head to the side, he ran his lips up the side of my neck. "Good, baby. Do you want to try something right now?"

With his hard length pressed up against me, his finger skimming up my center, and all that was Levi surrounding me, all the embarrassment I'd felt minutes before was gone. In its place was someone who definitely wanted to try something right now.

Because he'd let go of my hair slightly so that I could answer him, my nod was more visible this time.

I'd expected him to shut the shower off and for us to move through to the bedroom, so when he moved us so that we were directly under the spray instead, I was a bit disappointed.

Something which I felt stupid about seconds later when he instructed, "Put your hands flat against the wall and bend forward slightly."

Doing it, I dropped my head forward and watched the movements in his hand as he continued to run his finger through my folds. I was so focused on doing it that I didn't realize his other hand had joined it from the other side until his finger slowly pushed into me from behind, making me jump.

His hands stopped moving as he asked, "Am I hurting you?"

Shaking my head furiously, he chuckled and started up again, slowly moving his finger in and out of me as he circled my clit with the hand cupping my mound. Another thick digit joined the one inside me at the same time as he split the index and middle fingers of his other hand, using both of them either side of the bundle of nerves now.

Lifting my head, I turned it, feeling almost frantic with the need to kiss him. Correctly reading the movement, he was ready and swept his tongue into my mouth breathing as heavily as I was. Not once did he stop the movements of his fingers throughout the kiss, instead he increased the speed and friction until I was hanging by a thread.

143

And then he stopped. Just freaking stopped and removed both hands before he stepped away from me. Shooting him a shocked look over my shoulder, I watched as he picked up a foil packet and held it up to me.

"Boy Scouts. It pays to be prepared."

I sincerely doubted that they taught that in the Scouts, or that he'd been one.

All the shock from before left me when I heard the crinkling of the wrapper, and when he stepped back up behind me, I almost cried with relief. Notching the head of his cock at my entrance, he moved his other hand back to cup me between my legs.

"We're going to have frantic hair pulling sex where we're out of control one day, baby. But until you can verbally tell me if I'm hurting you, it's going to be more controlled," he growled, pushing into me slowly.

"Tonight, I'm being selfish because I want to feel your pussy squeezing me when you come this first time. I also want to feel it as I push slowly into your tight heat," he wiggled the fingers of the hand between my legs, and I realized he'd split them so that they were either side of his length so that he could do just that.

"But you will come," he rumbled, thrusting deep into me and making me gasp. Then taking a handful of hair again, he gently tugged my head back on his next thrust until I was looking up at the ceiling. "And I'm going to watch your face as it happens."

Withdrawing until just the tip of him was inside me, he plunged forcefully back into me. With the way my back was now arched, I felt every inch of his length as he moved inside me, and I noticed something I hadn't noticed last night – the ribbing on the condom he was using. It also meant that the underside of his shaft rubbed hard across the area inside of me that was directly connected to my clit, which he was now circling with the rough pads of his fingers, making me tighten around him even more.

Moving back so that there was some space between us, he let go of my hair. "Stay in that position, Lottie."

I couldn't have moved if I wanted to – which I sure as hell didn't. Keeping one hand in front of me so that he could continue circling the bundle of nerves there, he ran the other one slowly down my back until he got to the top of my ass.

The fact that he hadn't veered off to the side made me visibly tense up, and the relief that flooded me when his hand disappeared after it was…

Smack!

The sharp noise hit me before the realization that he'd spanked me did, but as soon as the nerve endings flared up and the sting sank in, I came hard, clamping down around him.

Through the spasms, I felt the fingers of the hand that had done it gripping my hip, and he groaned into my neck as he hit his own peak as he pressed into me as hard as he could.

It felt like the orgasm took all of my energy with it when it left, but somehow Levi managed to hold me up when I sagged, still panting.

Rubbing his hand over the area that he'd connected with, he kissed the center of my spine. "Did I hurt you?"

Apparently a killer orgasm was the cure to getting your voice back, because I managed to get out a slightly audible, "Fuck no!"

And to hell with me getting my throat checked before I spoke. The doctor obviously hadn't counted on sex with a Townsend being a factor when he gave that order, so he wasn't to know it would be impossible to follow it.

CHAPTER THIRTEEN

Levi

I t had been a week since anyone had seen Eric. We'd all survived Thanksgiving, no one died from the meat sweats, there were no arguments, no one was stabbed over the last piece of pie. It was almost normal.

Well, it would have been normal if my parents hadn't nervously broken the news to us that my cousins were coming for Christmas. Oh no, not the relatively normal ones, the fucking weird, abnormal, and the total anomalies to our DNA ones.

My dad's sister Veronica, aka Ronnie, lived in Florida with her husband Wyatt, and they had seven sons. It was a whole new ballgame when it came to them, so the news that they were coming wasn't exactly filling us all with joy – more like trepidation.

Even Gramps had said, "Hell no!" when they'd told him the news.

At least Lottie's voice was starting to come back, so she'd been

147

able to take part in conversations instead of writing shit down or just nodding. She'd been checked over briefly by Parker who'd agreed that she could talk unless it was painful, so now she got to use her new sexy, husky voice with us.

That was great news, and even better was that she wasn't allowed to go back to work until it was fully healed. I wasn't being an asshole on that, I just didn't know how we could keep her safe if she was at the hospital without one of us with her all the time.

I was currently going through the book she'd ordered on different positions to have sex in. I'm not going to talk about my past with her, it would be disrespectful, plus what happened before had no bearing on what I had with her now. But I can honestly say, I didn't know a lot of these existed. Now that I knew, though, I couldn't wait to try some of them out with her.

Looking up at her, I saw her frowning at the screen of her phone.

"What are you looking up, baby?"

Glancing up at me briefly, she swiped her thumb across the screen again, tilting it sideways. "Just an idea I had. It's not working out like I thought it would, though."

Her voice was still quiet and now came out in a husky rasp.

"It's not more positions, is it? Because, just to say, I'm almost certain all you'd have to do is talk to me or read me something, and that would be it for me."

That wasn't an exaggeration. Even my fucking brothers, Madix and Rich all gave her their full attention when she spoke, and it wasn't because they didn't want her to strain her voice. Yet another reason why the news of the impending visit from my cousins wasn't a good thing.

Snickering, she put the phone down beside her on the couch and looked at the book on my lap. "What, there aren't enough in there for you?"

There was, there absolutely was, but I hadn't needed a book for inspiration when it came to her. The night I'd spanked her and seen the pink handprint on her ass had been just the start. Initially, I'd been worried that I'd hurt her, but when she'd told me how much she'd enjoyed it, I'd started planning out what else we could do.

Now, with the help of this book, my mind was running on overtime trying to figure out what to do first.

Which gave me an idea. "Want to watch a movie with me later on?"

I didn't miss the look of disappointment on her face, she'd find out soon enough.

Anything that she was going to say back was stopped when a knock on the door interrupted us. Knowing it was one of the family, I pushed the book under the cushion I was sitting on and yelled out to them to come in. The door opened and Ariana and Luna entered, with Jamie on her hip.

Squealing when she saw her favorite uncle, I got up and walked over to her with my arms out. "There's my girl!"

Kids had always been anomalies to me, but the second Jamie was born something had just clicked inside me. Dahlia and Madix's son Shaw, and Tate and Lily's daughter Rebel had just made it click even more. I can't say I knew what I was doing, but I understood more than I thought I would and could do a hell of a lot more than I thought I'd be able to do. I'd even babysat them by myself on occasions, so I was an uncle pro.

"Did you know that Levi has an issue with music from the Levi's commercials?" Luna asked Lottie as she sat down beside her. "What was that song, Ariana? The one that we played all the time to piss him off?"

"*Inside* by Stiltskin?"

That was the beginning of twenty minutes of hell while they looked up which songs had been used in the commercials, going back as far as they could.

Jamie loved the Stiltskin song and was laughing and clapping with it, but whenever it was changed to something else, she'd start whining.

Standing up, I put her on my hip. "Ok, little traitor. We don't listen to that song, it's gross," I told her, gagging to make a point. She didn't look convinced, so sighing I started walking toward the den. "Wanna watch *Tangled* with me?"

Watching a kids' movie was like torture for me, but if it got me away from the hell they were putting me through? I'd watch them twenty-four hours a day.

Ever since I was little, I'd had the songs and even the brand itself thrown at me, so it was safe to say that I had a slight issue with it. People assume that it's cool to have a famous brand with your name on it, I can confirm that it sure as shit wasn't. And definitely not with my family.

Charlotte

The three of us watched him walk away, lecturing Jamie about why they didn't listen to the gross songs.

As soon as he was out of sight, Ariana leaned in. "What did you find?"

Making sure he was definitely gone, I whispered, "I contacted Banshee's breeder. They have two boys from their miniature litter still available to go home next week."

"You're getting two?" Luna asked looking shocked. "What if they turn out like Banshee?"

She had a point. Luna had two dogs, a big guard dog named Vlad, and a Daschund called Banshee, and he had that name for a reason – the dog howled and wailed more than Jamie did. Then there were Dahlia and Madix's dogs, a Chihuahua called Bing, and a Great Malamute called Harambe. Lily and Tate also had two dogs, a Deerhound called Chew Barka, and a Labrador called Ozzy Pawsborne...

It was only Archer who had one dog, Bogey, whose breath could be used as a military weapon. So, really, it was best that there were two of them, and these two were brothers so they knew each other.

I just hoped they were normal, like normal dogs were – not like Townsend dogs tended to be. Out of all of the family's dogs, I couldn't confidently say that any of them could be classed as anywhere near 'normal'. Then again, the names might be a good reason why.

Grabbing my hand, Ariana begged, "Just promise us you won't let Lily name them."

"Not a chance in hell."

The woman had threatened to call her baby Felullah Consuela Trixibelle when she was pregnant. When you looked at it like that, the name Rebel Rowser was a dream.

"Ok, email him back and say you'll take them. I'll speak to Noah, and we'll go and collect them next week," Luna planned excitedly. "Shit, we need to get puppy stuff."

And so began a new list in my notebook: PSP, aka Puppy Shit Planning. For the next hour, we bought stuff online which was going to be delivered to Ariana's house.

Did I forget to mention, she'd wanted a Daschund her whole life, but Levi had mixed her up with Luna and bought her Banshee instead. Ariana now had her beloved Daschy called Taser along with a Munchkin cat, so this was almost a form of revenge for her – getting Levi the dogs she always wanted, and got for someone else. Not that she was still bitter or anything.

"Now, we need to order the things for his actual Christmas presents," she whispered, grinning evilly at me. "They're in my eBay and Etsy carts."

Moving so she was sitting between us, she showed us the items she'd mentioned when I'd said that I wanted to get Levi a dog a couple of days ago. Apparently he had a strange dislike for cats, in that he avoided them – and even went as far as to walk out of his way to avoid them – so it had to be a pet of the canine species.

Not that I was judging by any standard, but a man of Levi's size walking with two miniature Daschunds? I couldn't wait to see it. I still hadn't recovered from seeing Madix walking Baileys last week. The little dog had stopped after a couple of minutes and yapped until he walked back, picked it up, and put it on his shoulder.

If Levi had to do that with his new babies… actually, I think my ovaries would explode.

Between the tree of us, Levi's Christmas presents were all bought, and the puppy stuff was on overnight order. I was nervous but excited about getting him the puppies, but he'd done so much for me that I wanted to give him something back.

As the girls were leaving and Jamie whining to get back to her Uncle Levi, Ariana threw over her shoulder, "Oh, by the way, Rich wanted to know if you could record the automated messages on the company's system. He says if people call and hear your voice, Townsend Oil will be a world famous entity."

"Tell that little bitch to shove it up his ass," Levi snapped, smiling apologetically at Jamie.

Unable to resist adding one last dig, she chuckled, "If you think that's bad, wait until the cousins get here."

I kept hearing them saying things like this, and I still didn't understand what was wrong with the cousins?

FOUR HOURS LATER...

When Levi had suggested that we watch a movie, I'd thought he'd want to watch something like an action film or maybe even a comedy.

He'd taken the cushions off the couch in the den and surprised me by pulling a bar that brought out a bed. Before I could lie down on it, though, he'd made me sit in the recliner while he brought through bedding, made the bed up, picked up the popcorn and snacks he'd put on the side in the kitchen, and had then lit some candles around the room. I'd been so caught up in watching it all that I hadn't seen him walking toward me until he was lifting me out of the chair and pulling my shirt over my head.

This led us to now, lying on the bed in our underwear with a thick, warm duvet over us. I was closest to the television with him behind me, which meant I had a closeup of the action on the screen.

Not that he'd chosen an action film. No, what he'd actually chosen was *Sliver*, which was basically soft porn. I hadn't seen the movie before, but I'd heard about it for sure.

His hand was in my panties as he dipped his finger in and out of me. "We need to get you an appointment with a doctor," he muttered.

Arching my back slightly, I reached over my head to bring his mouth closer to mine. "Why?"

With his lips skimming mine, he whispered, "I want to take you without a rubber."

This made my hand spasm where it was holding the back of his neck. In my mind, there were different levels in a relationship.

We'd spent so much time together as friends trying to work through my stupid bucket list that we'd had a good foundation by the time our relationship changed from friends to lovers.

Obviously sex was a very personal thing, at least to me it was considering he was the only person I'd done it with. And also obviously, I knew we were in a relationship together, there was no doubting that, but we'd never discussed it and having sex without a condom... it was a big step.

Raising his head to look down at me, he frowned. "You don't want that?"

Turning so that I was lying on my back, I tried to think of how best to say what I was thinking. It was slightly awkward considering where his hand was at that moment, but I wasn't about to add another level of awkwardness to the occasion by pointing that out.

"I know I don't have a lot of experience with relationships," I began, chewing on my lower lip, "but we've never discussed that before."

Jerking back slightly, he moved his hand out of my panties and rested it on top of them instead. "Having sex without a rubber?"

Sighing, I rubbed my face with my hands, I was tempted to just leave them over it while I said the rest, so I did. "I get that we're in a relationship, but sex without a condom... it's a different depth of relationship."

"Depth of relationship?" he repeated, sounding confused.

Peeking through the fingers of one hand I realized he was genuinely confused by it.

"Ok, so I'm about to make things very awkward then," I mumbled, wishing I'd just agreed to see Parker for the damned appointment. "What we have is a relationship, I get that."

"That's a relief."

"But what I'm saying is, not using a condom is a totally different type of... relationship," I cringed when I said the last word. I was totally screwing this up.

Before I could say anything else, he put his hand over my mouth and shook his head. "I'll take it from here. I'm thinking what you mean is that removing that barrier moves our relationship into a more long-lasting one and makes it deeper because of that. Am I right?" Not moving the hand away, he waited for me to nod my head and then lifted it up. "Thought so. Baby, you have to know that this between us is something I've never had before and is definitely something I don't want to lose."

"Well I do now."

His lips twitched when I whispered that to him, but he quickly went back to being serious. "I can promise you that I want to keep growing what we've started. I don't want to go back to a life that doesn't have you in it, so any chance I get to make it deeper, stronger, whatever, I'm going to do it."

Tilting my head to the side, I rubbed my thumb across the lines on his forehead where he was frowning. "Even if it means getting 'Lottie's bitch' tattooed on your forehead?"

"Even if it means getting that tattooed on my forehead," he chuckled. "So long as you get 'Levi's my master' tattooed on yours."

Pretending to think it over, I shook my head. "They might think I mean the jeans."

Dropping down to his back beside me, he scrubbed his face with his hands. "I hate that they told you that."

This time, it was me leaning on an arm and looking down at him. "You can't keep anything a secret, I'm afraid. The walls have eyes."

Dropping his hands, he grinned up at me. "Wanna give them something to talk about? Maybe we can put them in therapy with position seventy-two."

Holding a finger up, I reached behind me for my phone and opened up the messages. "One second, I've got an appointment to make with Parker."

That made him sit up straight in bed, yanking the warm duvet off me at the same time as he lunged at me. "I'm getting you raw?"

The look on his face was so intense that my mind went blank. "Raw?"

"Without a condom, baby."

It's strange how something like removing a piece of latex can mean so much to someone, but the emotions on his face showed that it was in fact a huge deal. It was to me, but I hadn't thought it would mean so much to him.

"Yeah."

Leaning down to give me a kiss, he murmured against my lips, "Tell him to see me at the same time. I'll get checked, you get covered, and then you're all mine."

Grinning, I typed out the request and set my phone down beside me. "What's position seventy-two?"

He did better than describing it to me, he showed me. And just to say, if the walls did have eyes, I was never looking at any of them ever again.

CHAPTER FOURTEEN

Levi

Four *days later...*

Lottie was going out on Night Rider again while I rode along on an ATV with Archer's dog Bogey.

Dad had a horse that was a cantankerous asshole, so Archer was going to ride him at the side of her. I wasn't sure who I felt worse for – me or him.

It was no exaggeration that Bogey had death breath, and no matter what it just never got better. Archer had taken him to the vet, he'd had his teeth cleaned, he ate the chews to get rid of bad breath, he had a special diet... that dog was born to kill people with one exhale. Which was why he was going in the back of the vehicle.

"Now, you remember what you're meant to do?" Archer asked as he checked all the straps on the saddle.

Nodding excitedly, Lottie reached down and scratched Night's ears, getting a happy grunt for her efforts. She was lucky she could ride after our appointments with Parker yesterday. That asshole had almost ended up with his stethoscope up his ass.

Now, as someone who'd never had sex with a condom and who'd always gone for his physicals and passed, I didn't expect him to pull out a swab and tell me he was going to stick it up my dick. I'd assumed it would be a run-of-the-mill blood test and then pee in a cup, but no. I wasn't sure how other men coped, but if he'd given me an anesthetic, I might have come out of it in better shape. It was like he'd stuck a fork up there and scraped it around.

Obviously, Lottie hadn't needed to get tested, but she'd been awesome when I'd come out limping. It was going to take a couple of days to get over it, and I had yet another reason to be relieved that I'd found Charlotte seeing as how I'd never have to go through it again.

Looking up, I watched as they took off at a slow trot and whistled for Bogey to jump up behind me. While they were riding, I was going to go through the list of options for what to get her for Christmas. Well, so long as the death breath being panted over my shoulder didn't kill me first.

THREE DAYS LATER...

"Parker's an asshole."

Looking up from the screen of his laptop, Archer raised his eyebrows. "Not got the results back yet?"

Shaking my head, I sat down in the chair on the opposite side of his desk. Looking around his office, I realized what was missing. "Where's the Gila monster?"

"The what?"

"Gila monster. It's a venomous lizard, how don't you know this?"

Still looking confused, he looked around his office. "I know what it is, but I don't get what you're talking about because I don't have one."

"Sure you do," I nodded over at the dog bed in the corner of his office. "He's got four legs, droopy ears, drools everywhere, and goes by the name of Bogey."

"He's not venomous, asshole," he snapped, throwing his pen at my head and hitting me in the beard.

"Respect the beard, pube face. And when was the last time you had his breath tested?"

Ignoring me, he went back to whatever was on his screen. Welp, I knew a cure for that. "Ok, I'll tell Bonnie you said hi when I see her at my house in... oh," I looked at my watch, "twenty minutes. Catch you later."

I only got as far as the door when he gave in.

"She's going to your house?"

"Yup," I threw over my shoulder, taking the corner in the direction of the exit to the office building we worked out of.

With everything going on with Lottie, I was lucky that it was so close to home and also that I could work from home. I rarely went to the drilling sites nowadays, I was more of the planning, permission, contracts and paperwork guy which I loved doing.

Just as I cleared the door, he came running up beside me and fell into step with me. I didn't have favorite siblings, but if I did, it would probably be Archer. Personality wise he was like Noah, but he was more closed off and a great listener. When he let his humor out, though, he was fucking hilarious. I just found it easy to be around him – and to wind him up.

Which I was going to do now.

"Where you headed?"

Shoving his hands in his pockets, he kept his eyes forward as he mumbled, "Figured I'd head and see if there was anything I could do to help out at yours."

"She said if you were there she wasn't coming."

Grabbing my shoulder, he turned me around to face him. "Is that what she said? Jesus Christ, I wasn't paying attention and when it happened it I wasn't expecting it, so I..." he stopped and squinted at me. "You're fucking with me, aren't you?"

Refusing to answer the question, I started walking again. "You'll have to wait and see."

"Wait," he called, jogging to catch up with me. "What does that mean?"

I wasn't sure, but I was hoping they'd made some popcorn. I wanted to see what was going to happen.

TURNED OUT, THE JOKE WAS ON ME. NOTHING SEEMED different when I walked through the front door. The girls were all sitting on the couches in the living room, but there were bags of shit everywhere.

Glancing at the top of one as I passed it, I frowned at the blue cushion poking out of the top. Blue? Where was she going to put blue?

The thing was, I didn't have it in me to even care if she did. She could change whatever she wanted, so long as I still had some green in my bedroom. And the den. And some out in the living room. Ok, so she could add some blue in with the green.

"You redecorating, Lottie?"

"No?" she rasped, looking at me like I was crazy.

Walking over to where she was sitting at the end of the couch, I sat down on the armrest and leaned into her.

"What's with the blue cushion then?"

That's when I heard it. Small scratching noises followed by what sounded like high pitched squeaks. Archer – who'd been discretely looking at Bonnie the whole time – heard it at the same time and looked around the room for the source.

"You guys got rats?"

Standing up, I looked around the room just as a tiny speck of brown dappled with white shot past my foot, followed by another one.

I dare any man to say he didn't do what I did, which was to get back on the armrest and lift my legs in the air.

Archer went a step further when he yelled and stepped up on the armrest closest to him – which just so happened to be Bonnie's and put his dick at the same height as her face. Oh, you bet your ass she looked.

"What the fuck is that?"

Watching the creatures with a smile on her face, Lottie sighed, "I've called them Burt and Ernie. Aren't they adorable?"

Looking up at my brother I saw a matching look of horror to the one I knew for sure was on my own face. "You bought yourself pet rats?"

Standing up, Ariana walked slowly over to where Archer was still balanced. "No, brother, she bought them for you."

This time, I aimed the look down at Lottie. "You bought *me* rats?"

I hated rats. I wasn't afraid of them, but they were nasty bastards who reproduced at an unnatural rate. When I was a kid, I was in the stables helping clean out the horses – one of the few times I ever did it – with one of Dad's friends. He was digging with his fork in the corner of the box when a freaking massive rat jumped out at him and he raised his fork just in time to protect himself. To this day I swear it was going to attack him, but it ended up impaling itself on one of the tines of the fork. At the time Ariana had a pet rat called Rastus, and I never looked at it the same way again. Ironically, Rastus escaped, so these might even be related to him.

Getting up, Lottie walked over to them and bent down to pick one up before I could stop her.

"They're not rats," she murmured, cradling it to her chest and walking back over to where I was sitting. "They're miniature Daschunds."

I started to lean backward as she held it out to me until this tiny little face peaked over her fingers and I saw what she was saying. As soon as it saw me, it tried to climb out of her hands to get to where I was sitting staring at the adorable little guy now. I'm a man, just a normal man, but inside I was kind of melting at the cuteness overload in front of me.

Reaching out to touch its ear, I chuckled when it quickly turned to lick my finger. "You should have told me you wanted a dog, Lottie. Wait, did you say you got two? Where did the other one disappear to?"

And there began the hunt for the missing Daschund. When it

didn't answer to everyone calling its name, we split up into teams and started searching inside and outside. It wasn't until an hour later when I was walking out of the second search in my den for it, that I heard little whimpers and found him underneath the couch.

I could only just get my hand under it, so I had to lift it up and balance it with one hand while I grabbed it with the other.

Holding him up in front of my face, I muttered, "How did you get under there?"

"Holy shit, you found it?" Archer rumbled behind me. "You need to call that thing Red October or something, because even Sean Connery couldn't have pulled that off."

"Hey, Lottie," Bonnie called, seeing us looking at the puppy who was now trying to lick my face. "We found him."

What Archer had suggested gave me food for thought. He did have reddish brown fur that was dappled with white like his brother's, and if my math was right he'd been born in October or thereabouts.

As Lottie joined us still carrying the other rug rat, I made my decision. "This is Red October, Red for short."

A frustrated noise from the doorway was followed by, "See what you've done, Lily? You've broken everyone with your weird names."

Not taking offense at what Ariana was saying, she just laughed. "I kinda like the name."

Now we just had to think up a new one for the other one. I was thinking Rambo.

CHAPTER FIFTEEN

Charlotte

I was sitting on the floor with Red and Rambo, watching them both pulling on the same little rope toy. It was like tiny canine tug of war.

"Don't you just love them?"

We'd only had them for three days, but in those three days I'd fallen head over heels in love with them. It was going to suck when Eric was caught and I had to go back to my own apartment. I'd get to see them and maybe I could babysit them on my days off, but it wasn't the same as having them around.

Running his finger down the middle of my forehead, Levi picked up on my change in mood. "What's causing that face?"

"Can I babysit them on my days off when I go back to my apartment?"

Pulling his hand back, he thought about what I'd just asked. "You can't go back, Lottie. Not while Eric's still hiding."

Yup, all of this time, all the people out there looking for him, and the ass breather still hadn't been caught. Somehow, through the haze of drugs in his system he'd managed to evade everyone. The guy couldn't stop himself getting caught fucking my best friend, but he could hide from the law?

I'd even called my parents one day and left a message to see if they could convince him to go home – where he'd be arrested by the police, but still – but they hadn't called back. Not that I'd really expected them to, but I'd explained what he'd done to me and I guess a part of me wanted them to care.

Seeing that Levi was still watching me, I pointed out, "But once he's caught, I will."

Chewing on his lip for a second, he mulled that over. "Do you want to go back?"

Did I? The simple answer was no. I didn't want to go back to not having him around, not having his family there to laugh with. I loved being around them, and I'd discovered that I really loved playing with the kids. I still wasn't sure what babies did exactly, but I was a pro at holding them now.

Initially Jamie had been wary of me, like she thought I was going to take her uncle away, but that had all changed now. Shaw was a little flirt and had immediately decided that I was his property. As soon as he heard me talking he started crying, and the second they passed him to me he stopped.

Out of all of them, Rebel was the easiest seeing as how she just slept and on the occasions when she was awake, she just wanted to look around the room and be nosy. But I was getting better with tiny humans, and I loved being around them all.

And I didn't want to not be able to see Levi like I could now.

Deciding to go with honesty, I sighed, "Not really, but it's where I live."

His reply was said so quietly that I almost didn't hear it. "Move in here."

"You want me to move in here?"

"I really want you to move in here," he corrected, picking up Rambo and holding him up in front of his face. "We all do."

Doggy blackmail... it was totally unnecessary. "Isn't it too soon?"

I already knew what his answer was going to be before he even said it. "Not even slightly."

My heart was racing as I thought about actually living with Levi officially. Nothing that he owned was of any significance to me, I didn't care about material things. What I cared about was sitting right in front of me, offering me the chance to make it official. Only a crazy person would be able to say no to that, and I definitely wasn't crazy.

"How would it work?"

Getting up, he walked over to me and stopped when there were only a matter of inches between us, meaning that I had to tip my head all the way back to look at his eyes.

"We'll sort that out when the time comes," he whispered, pulling me up onto my feet in front of him. "Now, are you moving in with me?"

Like he has to ask me twice. Not even thinking about it, I threw my arms around his neck. "Yes, I'll make honest puppies out of them."

Bursting out laughing, he picked me up and spun me through the air, making Red and Rambo start yapping at us.

"I'm fairly certain this isn't an appropriate time to be laughing, but I couldn't care less."

Grinning down at him, I warned him, "I'm fairly certain what I do next isn't a standard response either, but I don't give a damn!" And threw my arms up in the air, making him laugh even harder.

Somehow, through his stomach bouncing me as he laughed, me being a dork, and two tiny dogs now yanking at the hems of his pants, he managed to lower me without dropping me until I had my legs wrapped around his waist and we were face to face. Slowly the smile disappeared as he watched me, like he wanted to say something, making me tense up.

"If we're going to go on certainties, I'm definitely certain I don't like that look on your face right now," I mumbled, hoping he'd go back to smiling, but he didn't. In all the time that I'd known him, I'd never seen him looking like this, and it worried me.

"I know I want to say something, but I'm not sure if it's the right thing to say."

Taking a deep breath in, I tried to lighten the mood. "I know," I pointed at myself, "that you know," I shifted so that my finger was now pointing at him instead, "that you can say anything you need to, to me. You know?"

Chewing on his lip for a second, he shifted his eyes to the side, and then looked back at me. "I'm definitely certain that I love you, Lottie."

I'd been bracing myself for him saying he'd changed his mind or that he'd been hiding a sixth toe, so initially the words didn't register but the relief sure as hell did.

"Is that it? That's what made you look like you were…" I trailed off, replaying the words in my head. "Wait, you love me?"

Narrowing his eyes, he started walking, ordering the two dogs to go to their bed – which they did, surprisingly. I was so dumbfounded by what he'd just said and was still staring at his nose when he started lowering me down, that it was a shock when I realized I was now sitting on the edge of the bed.

"Now," he drawled, bending down into me and gently pushing me onto my back. "I know, that you know, that I said I love you. So I now know that you know." With each word his mouth got closer to mine, but I had something to say now so I covered it with my hand.

"Know what I know?" I whispered, waiting for him to shake his head. "I know that I've never loved anyone as much as I love you, and I've never felt more like I belong somewhere in my life. I know that I want to stay here, because I belong here, but I also know that I won't ever feel like this with anyone but you." As I finished saying it, I lowered my hand away and kept my focus on his mouth.

What I should have been doing was looking at his eyes which were now back to being narrow slits as he glared at me, but it had to be said that it was done with a good dose of humor, too.

"You know," he growled, "it took me a long time to figure out how to say those words to you, and you just had to go and beat me, didn't you?"

And this was why I belonged here. He understood me, he totally got me, and knew that if it had stayed serious I would have been out of my depth. I knew he loved his family, but I didn't know if he'd ever given a declaration of love to a woman outside of it.

What I did know, as did Levi, was that I'd never told my family that I loved them or heard it back from anyone - this was the first time I'd ever given that to someone - so it would have been easy to become overwhelmed by it. Something like that shouldn't happen at a moment like this but it could happen, and he was doing his best to help me avoid it. No one deserved to have the memory of a moment like this darkened by something like that, because it was a moment I wanted to look back at for the rest of my life as the best one I'd ever had. Actually, that was a lie – since he'd come into my life and we'd started hanging out, every one of the best moments of my life had involved him, this was just the cherry on top. Something that I decided to tell him.

"I haven't had a bad life," I started, shaking my head when I saw him looking like he was going to argue about that with me. "No, Levi, I haven't. I've had an education, I had a good home, I had food, I had almost everything I needed. I just didn't have the family that a child needs…"

"You were surrounded by people who were manipulating and controlling you, Lottie. That isn't under the definition of a 'good life'," he pointed out.

"Yeah, but I was safe and looked after even with all of that."

"You call what your parents set up with Eric safe?"

I couldn't help wincing at that, he had a good point. "Ok, aside from him. He was the exception to the safety aspect."

"You call parents who didn't personally involve themselves in your life as safe, too?" he pressed. "Baby, I'm not trying to hurt you by bringing this up, I'm trying to make you see it for what it was."

Which I could understand, but he needed to understand it too. "I know that, but remove your emotions for now and look at it from my perspective. You saw what Luna went through firsthand," I reminded him, hating the sadness that the words brought him. "That wasn't a good life or being safe. Now look at what I had, it's very different. But I can say for sure that every single one of the best moments of my life have been since I met you, and that they've all involved you."

Pressing down so that I had to widen my legs for him to lie in between, he stroked my cheek with his thumb. "I wasn't with you while you were riding Night Rider."

"Yes, you were. You were standing there each time and then you followed on the ATV with Bogey when we went on the long ride."

As soon as I mentioned the dog's name, his face scrunched up slightly. "That dog's breath is just damn awful," he muttered and then went back to thinking. "I wasn't with you when you got Red and Rambo."

"No, but I bought them for you and with you in mind the whole time. In fact, I was excited because I was picturing your reaction when you saw them."

"And I thought they were rats," he chuckled, shaking his head.

Um, not quite. "No, you thought I was going to mess up your green with blue cushions at first," I reminded him, grinning when he looked surprised. "Yup, I can read you that well."

Moving so that his crotch pressed more firmly against mine, he kissed me gently. "You can, can you? And what am I thinking now?"

That was easy to answer, I could feel what he was thinking seeing as how it was hard and pressed against me.

Shifting my hips so that I pressed up against his hardness, I whispered, "Something related to one of the positions in the book you've stolen from me."

I hadn't even had a chance to do more than skim some of the pages in it before he'd taken it away from me.

Shaking his head, he leaned down and kissed me again. "That's where you're wrong. I'm actually thinking of a phone call I got while you were in the shower earlier."

A phone call? "What?"

"Uh-hum," he hummed, grinding down against me. "A phone call, one that I've been waiting for."

What the hell kind of phone call was he talking about? Then it clicked. "Parker!"

"That's right. And with me having the all clear and you having the injection a week ago, guess what?"

I didn't need to guess what, every part of my vagina was screaming at me what was what. So, I used his word back at him making him groan. "Raw."

No other words needed to be said as he raised up to pull my top over my head, followed by his own. The thing was, not only had I ordered stuff for the dogs to be delivered to Ariana, but I'd also placed an order at a shop they knew where Levi's cousins lived called Scarlett Temptations. And I'd put the first set that had arrived on this morning.

He'd only just dropped his t-shirt behind him when he noticed the lace bra that was in a purple-blue color. "Holy shit."

"You tear it, I'll kill you," I warned him, lifting my hands up to undo the clasp at the front myself, and frowning when he knocked my hands out of the way gently.

Shaking his head, he lowered the tip of his finger to skim it along the outside edge of the lace, stopping on the little clip at the front holding it together.

"I really love this, and I want to be the one to take it off."

Expecting him to do just that, I was confused when he leaned over and ran his tongue where his finger had just been instead. That was until he moved down slightly and sucked my nipple through the lace. Hissing, I held his head, arching my back slightly at the same time.

"Jesus, why does that feel so good?"

Either he didn't know or he was too involved in what he was doing, because he just moved across to the other side to do the same thing there. Not that I had it in me to care, at this precise moment words were cheap if you asked me. So, I ran my nails down his back, groaning when it made him grind down into me again as he continued moving his mouth over my breasts.

Not one to stay idle, I moved my right hand around the front of his jeans and worked one handed to undo the button and zipper on them so that I could fit my hand down to where his hard cock was. That said, I wasn't going to make it easy on him so I pulled on all of my self-control, and did it as slowly as possible, torturing him with the anticipation just like he was doing to me.

Finally, freaking finally, I had it in my hand and did my best to wrap my fingers around it.

"Tighter," he rasped, and I almost groaned with relief when he undid the damn clasp.

Doing as he'd asked, I tightened my grip and started moving my hand up and down as well, while he lifted up to get to the zip on my jeans, unveiling the matching panties to the bra. As soon as he saw them, he reared up jerking his cock out of my hand, and yanked the pants off my legs.

"This color," he whispered, running his hands up my thighs toward where he was staring between my legs. "And this pussy…" he said, grunting as he cupped me between my legs now and looked up at me. "Photos of it need to be under the definition of perfection."

Ignoring his earlier order, I sat up to pull the bra straps down my arms and throw it to the side.

"I'd rather they weren't," I breathed, falling back down flat on the bed when he pulled the crotch of the panties to the side and swept a finger down the center of my lips.

Shaking his head, he blew out a breath. "I don't know if I can do this slowly, Lottie. I need you too badly."

That I could understand, if he was feeling as overwhelmed by it all, by what we were about to do for the first time, as I was... it was too much. Slowly wasn't a factor that was possible, it needed to happen now.

"I don't want slow, Levi. I need you inside me now."

Those words opened the floodgates – well, the panty gates seeing as how he managed to get mine off my legs in a matter of seconds and was then moving us further up the bed.

As soon as he had us where he wanted us to be, he was kissing me, his tongue exploring my mouth at the same time as his hand moved down to my pussy. On the first skim of his finger through my center, he groaned into my mouth at the same time as my hips jerked up toward him.

"It drives me fucking crazy knowing that you're all mine, and that I'm going to make love to you on *our* bed."

Reaching up to hold his face, I felt a shift inside me. I hadn't thought of it as ours, he was the one who owned everything in the house, but now that I was moving in he was right – we'd be sleeping on the bed, living together inside the property, sharing it all. It was ours. And that made me think of the fact that I hadn't contributed anything toward it, and I needed to fix that soon.

Before I could say anything, though, two of his fingers slowly pushed into me and any thoughts and concerns not related to what we were doing right now disappeared. In fact, pretty much everything disappeared including my ability to keep my eyes open or hold my head in place.

With my head now tipped to the side, I jumped when I felt the brush of his beard on my nipple and couldn't hold back the moan that came out of me when it moved back and forth over it.

That was something they didn't put on the beard t-shirts, that it would drive your woman out of her mind when you rubbed it across her pussy and nipples. Someone should really do that, because then more women would see the true beauty behind their man having one. False advertizing and misrepresentation - the beard version.

At the same time as his mouth closed around the nipple that his beard had just been tormenting, he withdrew his fingers and replaced it with the blunt head of his cock and started to push the hard length into me. The difference a thin piece of latex made was instantly noticeable, and apparently he thought the same thing.

Stopping halfway, he dropped his head onto my chest, shaking slightly. "Fuck, I'm never going to last. This is... it's... fuck."

Taking a couple of deep breaths, he raised his head back up again, and I was able to see how tense his face was. Digging my nails into his back, I wrapped my legs around his hips and started to pull him further into me, his eyes shooting open and staring at me in shock.

"I need more."

Those three words broke whatever control he had, because he pushed back against my legs, withdrawing from me until just the tip was still inside, and then plunged back in until his full length was buried deep inside me making both of us shout at the same time.

Rising up so that he was balanced with his arms straight, he began to thrust into me harder and faster. The distance between us allowed me to look down and see his bare cock as it disappeared back inside me, and seeing where I was looking, he looked down, too.

"Jesus Christ," he groaned, thrusting back in harder, both of us still watching it.

The shaking in his arms showed how hard he was holding back, so I reached down and started rubbing my clit, immediately clenching down on him as soon as I skimmed the bundle of nerves.

"Shit!"

Dropping down onto one arm, he used the other to scoop up one of my legs so that my knee was supported by it, and he pushed it closer to my body. The change in angle tipped me over the edge and I cried out, digging my nails into his back as I spasmed around his length.

Losing the strength in his arm, he lowered down slightly and groaned as pounded into me, pushing my knee even closer to my chest. Just as I started to come down from my orgasm, he hit his own and exploded inside me. Of course I knew that it would feel different, but never in my wildest dreams had I thought it would feel this different. I could feel every pulse so much more clearly. I could feel everything as he came inside me.

Evidently, Levi felt the same way because once his brain went back online, he opened his eyes and rasped seriously, "You are everything. There just isn't a better word for to describe it. Every second that I've spent with you has been the best second of my life. And what we just did? I'll never be able to find the words to explain what it did to me."

I kinda could. Slapping his ass weakly, I panted, "We need to do that again. Now."

CHAPTER SIXTEEN

Levi

Two weeks later...

All I'd done was walk through the door after meeting with my brothers in the office to discuss a contract I was working on. I'd been thinking about the contract as I'd entered the house, double checking that I'd bought my Christmas presents for everyone, wondering how soon the guy painting the den with the new color of paint would be finished – innocent shit like that.

Basically, I'd been preoccupied, but the second I'd opened the door I'd been faced with Lottie's ass as she balanced on her hands and knees, playing with Red and Rambo.

Christmas disappeared, the contract was shredded, I didn't give a shit about paint... But I did give a shit about the painter, especially seeing as how all I could see was my hoodie and her panties.

"Where's the asshole?"

Looking over her shoulder, she rolled her eyes at me. "I wish you wouldn't call your dad that."

Potato – potahto, he'd interrupted us this morning, so he'd more than earned the name.

Looking around for a blanket to put over the pink lace covering her delectable cheeks, I frowned when I didn't hear Dad anywhere.

"Is he in the bathroom? I hate it when he uses my toilet, he fucks around with the toilet paper, moves shit around…"

"He finished the walls," she snickered, stopping me mid-rant. "Do you want to go and see?"

Looking back down at the lace with a hundred ideas hitting me all at once, I walked slowly toward her shaking my head.

"Not even slightly," I growled, dropping down to my knees behind her. Raising my hand, I skimmed it up the inside of her thigh, leaning over her shoulder to give her a kiss and ignoring the little canine shithead who was trying to lick my face. "What I want to do is…"

A sudden pounding at the door made both of us jump. Glaring at it over my shoulder, I bellowed, "*We're busy.*"

Yeah, I was grouchy. I'd had Charlotte wrapped around me this morning, slowly kissing down my stomach, when Dad had turned up. I hadn't even been able to have a shower with her and I loved showering with her in the mornings.

Hell, he wouldn't even let me kiss her goodbye because he wanted French toast and Mom wouldn't let him have it, so he was extorting it out of Lottie. It might seem stupid to be hung up on such small things, but I loved the time we spent together and the routine we had going. In the all too near future she'd be going back to work and our relationship would move into a different stage. We'd also be in a more comfortable relationship which didn't feel as new as they did now, so those moments might get fewer and further between, so I was getting as many in now as I could.

Plus, maybe there was something to this theory about the man period, because I was cranky as fuck just now and felt achy. Which might give me a good defense in court when they asked why I killed the person still trying to break my door down.

"You can't say that," Lottie hissed, pushing me away from her while she tried to get to her feet.

"Sure I can. It's our house, and we were busy," I replied unrepentantly, reaching for her just as the soon-to-be dead person on the other side of the door hammered hard enough to rattle the hinges. "Fuck. Off!"

The voice that replied was an unknown to Lottie making her frown, but it was definitely a known one to me. "You're really not going to let your favorite cousin in?"

The way my head fell back until I was looking up at the ceiling was a natural reaction, and a justified one. "Ah, fuck no."

Leaning in close to me, Lottie whispered, "Who's your favorite cousin?"

Raising my head back up so I could show her how serious I was, I muttered, "None of them. They're all a pain in the ass."

What was most likely a boot hit the door. "You know, your door isn't as soundproof as you think."

"It was until you tried kicking it in," I yelled, getting to my feet and pulling Lottie to hers with me, before tearing open the door to face him.

Sure enough, there stood my cousin Elijah, all six feet and six inches of him with his arms braced on my door frame, and the world's most irritating grin on his face.

Straightening up, he held his arms open wide, "Cousin."

Thankfully, Lottie had run to put some pants on so I didn't have that to worry about, but Red and Rambo took full advantage of the open door to try to escape. I managed to grab Red before he got too far, but Rambo ran past a confused Elijah and started trying to get down the steps.

"Catch him, will you?"

Holding his hands out in front of him, he shook his head wildly. "I don't touch vermin, man. I need to keep my tools clean and all."

A hand pushed me out the way and Lottie ran out after Rambo – thankfully with pants on now. Scooping him up, she turned back and stopped when she came face to face with Elijah's chest. Almost like it played out in slow motion, she slowly looked up his chest until she reached his face and stared at him.

"Elijah, this is Lottie. Lottie, this is…"

Not waiting for me to finish, he held his hand out to her. "Elijah Townsend-Rossi, his favorite cousin."

Shaking his hand, she smiled at him and looked nervously over at me. "Great to meet you. I didn't know you were coming today."

Flicking a wide-eyed glance at me as soon as he heard her voice, he replied smoothly, "I wanted to surprise this one. Gotta say, though, hearing that voice and seeing how beautiful you are, I don't blame him for not opening the door." Clenching my fists, I started rehearsing my apology to my aunt over the death of her son, when he turned his head fully in my direction. "You lucky fucking bastard."

Trying to ease some of the tension, Lottie took her hand back from where he was still holding it and smiled at both of us. "This is so awesome. When are your brothers arriving?"

Rolling my eyes, I opened the door all the way and stood back. "No one knows when they're coming, they just turn up."

Some might think I was being rude, but it was true. In fact, I had good reason to not be happy with Elijah and he knew it, which he proved by bursting out laughing.

"You still pissed at me? Come on, I thought we were friends."

Shooting him a glare, I closed the door behind them, trapping the two puppies which were now pulling on his shoelaces and growling. If it had been anyone but him I'd have told them off... No, wait, I was totally lying. If it had been one of a handful of people I'd have done that, but definitely not with him.

"What did you do?" Lottie asked, unable to help herself.

"I sent him a cake for his birthday," he shrugged, sitting down on the couch and watching Red and Rambo. "What are they?"

"Miniature Daschund puppies. What was wrong with the cake?"

"It was one of those diaper cakes. It was actually a total fluke that they had denim diapers out at the time, and also that you can buy fake Levi jeans labels online."

Yeah, I was pretty certain you weren't meant to do that and with his job breaking the law wasn't just frowned upon – it was a fuck no. Which obviously I reminded him about, because I'm a good cousin and all.

Waving it off, he looked at me and for the first time, I saw how tired he was. I wasn't a heartless bastard, I might still have a tiny bit of a grudge (what he'd divulged to Lottie didn't even come close to what he'd done), but I actually loved my cousins no matter how big of a pain in my ass they were. Seeing the guy who always seemed like he didn't have a care in the world trying to hide something that was big enough to smother that carefree attitude? It concerned me.

"Speaking of work, how's it going?"

"Busy." That was it, that was all he said. I left it a second to see if he'd expand on it, but he purposely kept his eyes on the dogs.

"What do you do, Elijah?" Lottie asked him this time as she curled up and leaned into my side.

With anyone else, he would probably just ignore the question, but he looked up and saw the way we were sitting and his eyes softened. "I'm in the Coast Guard in Alaska."

"Whoa, that's really cool. Are you on a ship or do you go on the helicopters?"

"Both. We land on the ships periodically to launch off of, but usually it's from land."

Saving her from having to wring the answers out of him, I cleared my throat. "Elijah is the guy who goes down into the water, or lowers from the helicopter onto the deck, baby. He's a rescue swimmer."

"You go into the water in Alaska? How are you still alive?"

Smiling at her, he replied, "We try not to spend too much time in the water when we go down."

"Do you have a survival suit?" When he nodded, she asked the question that I'd figured was coming. "Can I try it on? How warm does it keep you?"

Sitting back, I watched as she threw question after question at him – some he dodged, some he answered. There were also a couple of internet searches to look up what he'd mentioned and most of those triggered more questions, too. At one point, he looked up at me like he was begging for me to help him, but I just shot him one of his shit-eating grins back making it clear no help would be forthcoming from this cousin. The grudge – it was real.

Finally, when she'd run out of questions, I repeated my earlier question, phrasing it nicely this time. "So, how come you came earlier than the others?" Before he could answer it, I followed it with an almost paranoid, "It is just you, isn't it?" And looked around us like more of them were standing behind me.

"Yeah, the others aren't due for a couple of days, but I heard you had some problems going on and figured I'd come lend a hand."

Sighing, I groaned, "And who told you I had problems?"

Bursting out laughing, he leaned forward to pick Red up, holding him in front of his face like he was trying to make sure he was of the canine species and not a rat. "Gramps did."

Covering my hands with my face, my initial instinct was to scream into them but that would make me look like a little bitch. "Fuuuuuck."

The bark of laughter that came out of Elijah didn't help the frustration and sinking in my gut. If Gramps had told him, it meant he'd told all of them. That meant that they'd also try to come early, some of them letting us know they were here, the others not doing that. Instead, they'd just get stuck into finding Eric and it would all go to hell.

I had two cousins who were twins, Jackson and Marcus, and they were the worst for it. The last time they'd tried to help out, they'd planted a booby trap near the lake that was on our property, and had blown up five trees. Incidentally, they also blew up the ATV that they'd been riding at the time, having forgotten where they'd set the booby trap and only jumping off at the last second when they saw the wire.

Charlotte's eyes were huge as I told her all of this, and she looked at Elijah in a new light when she looked back at him.

"That's crazy!"

Not taking any offense at her saying that about his brothers – not that he could – he nodded his head. "Yup, but I can't say that the rest of our family are known for being normal."

"None of us have ever blown anything up."

"Yeah, but some of you have accidentally hit the trigger on the shotgun," he pointed out, talking about when Tate was a kid. He'd totally done that, and probably would now, which was why we made it clear that he wasn't to touch the big guns. Nerf guns, sure. Real guns, he couldn't be trusted with. Looking at Lottie, he tilted his head as he took her in. "You ever shot a gun, honey?"

I felt her turn to stone under my hand, and she shifted uncomfortably. "Uh, no. I've never needed to."

"You stay with this one," he nodded at me, "you're gonna find you need to. It's safer, trust me. Either that or you'll want to shoot a gun – at him."

And just as I'd been softening toward him, he levelled back up to total asshole.

CHRISTMAS DAY...

Ever wondered what total anarchy and chaos looks like? It was Christmas day with my family. There was paper everywhere, boxes spilling out the items that had been wrapped in them, people excitedly talking as they played with their presents and ate the little snacks that Mom had put out. This year, the sound of obnoxious music and the loud noises coming from the kids' presents joined it all, too.

Holding out the tray with deviled eggs on it to Lottie, I popped one in my mouth. "Egg, baby?"

It was almost like I'd asked her if she wanted to shove the tray up her ass the way she moved quickly away from it. "No, I don't eat eggs."

Seeing the pink on her cheeks, I leaned into her. "Why would that be?"

Not making eye contact with me, she mumbled, "I'm allergic."

She was lying. "Allergic?" I asked skeptically. "But you eat food with eggs in them."

"No, I don't."

"Pasta, mayo, you had pancakes yesterday, you ate egg rolls at dinner last night, donuts, French toast, potato salad," I listed, thinking over the foods I remembered her eating with an egg in them.

Wincing as I listed them all, she looked around us like she was looking for help. "I was being polite?"

Pulling her into my front, I turned her head so that she was looking up at me. "What's the real reason you won't eat a deviled egg, Lottie? And no more lies."

I don't think I'd ever seen someone blush as hard as she was at that moment. "I don't think we're at the stage in our relationship where we can discuss this sort of thing, Levi."

I'd been determined to find out the real reason before, but now it was a matter of life and death. "Lottie."

Shoving her head into my chest, she grabbed two handfuls of my top and tried to wrap them around her head. "Lottie, tell me."

Because she didn't lift her head out of where it was, her answer was muffled and I had to strain to hear it. But I heard it, oh sweet Jesus did I hear it. "Some egg dishes react violently with my stomach, ok?"

Bursting out laughing, I pulled my shirt off her head. "React violently? What the hell is that?"

Elijah and Archer walking up saved her from answering. "What are y'all talking about? Merry Christmas by the way, Charlotte," Elijah told her, giving her a wink and then looking up at me when he saw how red she was. "Holy shit, what did you say to her?"

Grabbing me by the beard, she pulled my head down until my face was about an inch away from hers. "You tell them, and I swear they'll never find your penis."

"Jesus," Archer muttered, taking a step back.

"And I'll put hair removal cream in your beard."

Closing that inch until my nose was touching hers, I growled, "You wouldn't dare."

My penis was one thing, but a man's beard was sacred.

"Shit, she went for his beard. That's Levi-sacrilege," Elijah whispered to Archer.

"True story, he was born with that thing," he agreed, looking between the two of us.

"She might have issues finding that penis, though."

Raising my head back up to glare at them, I snapped, "Will the two of you shut up? Don't you have other people to piss off?"

Rocking back on his heels, Elijah scratched his belly absentmindedly as he looked around the room. "Nope, we're waiting for the brothers to get here. Apparently there was an accident so they're held up in traffic."

Spinning around, Lottie clapped excitedly. "Wait, they're on their way? Why didn't you say? I need to make sure my phone's got a good amount of battery."

Frowning at her, Elijah asked, "Why do you need that?"

Seeing as how she was already moving to where her coat was on the couch, the question was asked to the back of her head. Still, she answered it, making me and Archer burst out laughing.

"Because if they're anything like you, the videos are going to make me rich."

Fucking right!

Charlotte

Every single bone in my body hurt. I'd never been part of a Christmas celebration like it, and I was going to have to start going to the gym now to survive next year.

It had started normally, with everyone exchanging presents like *normal* people do. Then they'd started passing around the food – little things to nibble on to start with, some chips and dip, normal things like that.

For dinner, we'd all sat down at the table and Erica had brought out four of the biggest turkeys I'd ever seen in my life with platters of vegetables and sides.

During it, Elijah had started the nurse questions, the ones every nurse loves to be asked.

"What's the weirdest thing you've ever seen stuck in someone's body?" I'd seen a lot, but the answer had to be a bullet, followed by a butt plug made out of Lego.

"Have you ever had a patient with a hamster up their ass?" No.

"Have you ever seen a patient with glass up their ass?" Yes, a beer bottle.

"How does someone get a vibrator stuck inside them?" Bad luck and poor planning.

"What's the biggest thing you've ever seen stuck up an ass?" A large shampoo bottle, and one of those huge jars of peanut butter.

"What do you do with the stuff you pull out?" It's up to the patient.

It had been endless, and by the time they were distracted by dessert, I was relieved that Elijah's brothers hadn't arrived yet because I had a feeling it would have gone on for longer.

And the dessert, oh those poor pies. Unfortunately, those had been made by Luna and Dahlia who had both decided that it would be less of a pain in the ass if they had some wine before they did it. Wine ended up as sex on the beach which was technically just vodka because they didn't have the other ingredients, apparently. So, doing shots of vodka – in normal water glasses because they didn't have shot ones – they made some pies.

Thanks to a lot of the vodka and a little of the tequila, they mixed up cream with sour cream, sugar with salt, and didn't add butter into the base. What we got was a base that was ground crackers only so it disintegrated when you touched it and the most god awful tasting pies.

Bad, right? Well, they'd also made a mousse in case people didn't want pie – squirty cream and cocoa powder. When it got to the table, it looked like diarrhea.

Because there was no dessert, people decided they'd have a drink to finish off the meal and raided Erica and Jerome's liquor cabinet.

I'd left early, but they were all still drinking when I did – more than likely to numb their taste buds after the mouthful of pie we'd all tried out of politeness. Biggest mistake ever, I'd rather take my chances with deviled eggs.

It had been a long week, and it was only Thursday, so no one had taken it badly when I'd bowed out before the rest of them. The truth was, I wanted to try to call my parents. It was Christmas and even though they hadn't replied to my last message about Eric, a part of me was certain that they'd answer today. I mean, it was freaking Christmas day!

Just as I was about to hit their number, my eyes caught on the present that Dahlia, Lily, and Luna had given me earlier – the one they'd told me I couldn't open until I got home. In fact, they'd almost panicked when I'd said it would be ok and had started opening it in front of them.

Putting my phone to the side, I picked it up and gave it a shake. Nothing made that tinkly broken glass noise when I did it, but there was some heavy thudding.

Making sure I was alone, I ripped off the paper and frowned at the brown box that was under it. If you were going to give someone a gift that was secretive, wouldn't the nice thing to do be to at least make it something in a box that told you what it was when you took the paper off? They'd made me hide this under my coat like it was porn or something.

Oh shit, they hadn't got me a box set of porn, had they?

Biting my lip, I argued with the stupid tab thing that was holding it shut, and then lifted up the lid. What was inside wasn't anything I'd seen before. It looked like a short rocket ship in different sizes with weird bumps and arms coming out of some of them. I recognized the next item in the box, a vibrator, but it had something else attached to it that stuck up in the air, too.

Removing those items from the box, I put them on the floor beside me and picked up a package with different tubes in it and read the labels out loud.

"Cherry lube, apple lube, Baileys lube, warming lube, ice fire lube, tingling lube... how many types can you get?" Considering there was two rows of five in the package, I'm thinking the answer was a lot.

Placing it down next to the others I'd already taken out, I lifted out the next thing. A vibrating cock ring. Turning it over, I wasn't sure whether to wince or laugh at the images on the back that told you how to use it. The item that was next to it in the box also said it was a cock ring, but this one was thick and made of black rubber.

By the time I got to the bottom of the box, I was kinda turned on, definitely curious, and absolutely embarrassed. There was also some hilarity and laughter, but holy shit those girls had no shame. They'd added in nipple clamps, a clit clip with a dangling diamond, another butt plug that was metallic with a diamond at the end, a row of beads that were apparently also for your butt, a clit vibrator, and finally the last thing had been a prostate massager. Seeing as how I definitely didn't have one of those, I was taking it that this one was a gift for Levi.

Leaning over the pile of sex toys, I went to pick up my phone when I heard something breaking in the living room.

Standing up, I opened the door and headed toward where the noise had come from calling out, "Red, Rambo, if you've broken something special, your daddy's gonna..."

That was kind of the last thing I got to say because an arm went around my throat from behind me, and something was placed over my face.

Of course both of those things made me scream into the rag on my face, but it was the voice that whispered, "Merry Christmas, Charlotte. I can't wait to give you the present I got you," that made me hyperventilate just as I lost consciousness.

CHAPTER SEVENTEEN

Levi

"I need to ask her this question," Elijah insisted, pushing past me as we walked through the dark living room toward the bedroom. "It's such a good one."

Ironically, the fact that the house was dark didn't really strike me as strange. Lottie tended to turn lights off as she went, but normally not unless I was with her. Given how busy the day had been, it wouldn't have surprised me if she'd just come home and passed out.

Archer had been the one who'd walked her back saying that Bogey needed to go potty, and I knew he'd stick close to the house to keep an eye on her while we waited for my cousins to arrive. Only two of them had, though, Webb and Jesse, because the others had taken the route that was blocked by the accident.

When I walked into the bedroom and saw the bed made neatly and the bathroom light on, *that's* when I realized something wasn't right. Lottie would never go to the toilet with the door open in case I came home, and she would have crawled into bed by now or called out when she heard us if she wasn't in it.

Panic that she'd fallen and hurt herself hit me as I walked into the bathroom. What I saw on the floor wasn't at all what I expected, though.

"Hey, did you know there's a broken... Whoa, Levi," Elijah clapped me on the back. "I never knew y'all had it in you. That's quite a collection."

Crouching down, I picked up the wrapping paper and the tag next to it.

HERE'S TO HAIR PULLING, BUTT SPANKING, SHMEXY SEX.
MERRY CHRISTMAS!
LOVE, LILY, LUNA AND DAHLIA XXX
PS WELCOME TO THE FAMILY.

Reading it over my shoulder, Elijah muttered, "Can't say I'm surprised it's from them. They got me cock soap and this thing to keep my balls warm."

Those had been his gag gifts and we'd all gotten something like that. Well, aside from my parents who were still feeling victimized by the fact they hadn't gotten anything filthy.

Turning around, I broke into a jog as I moved around the house looking for her. "Lottie! Where are you?"

Between the two of us, we had every room checked and every light in the house on within minutes.

"I'm not sure if this is related, Levi," Elijah said as he tried to catch his breath. "But there's a window in the bedroom at the back that's broken."

Running through to the room, I screeched to a halt on the

wooden floors when I saw the grass and dirt on top of the glass, with muddy footprints leading out of the room.

"Fucking shit," I yelled at Elijah. "Call everyone and tell them we need vehicles, guns, and lights. Tell Dad to call Barron and Connor and tell them that Retter's here and he's got Charlotte."

Pulling his phone out of his pocket, he rang straight through to Dad and started relaying the message while I grabbed my torch and went outside. There was an old shed about forty yards from my house, so I ran over to it and almost tripped over the body in dark clothing lying in the grass. It was too big to be her, but I turned it over and yelled out for Elijah when I saw the blood running down Archer's face.

"Elijah, tell them we're at the old shed and that Archer's hurt."

Confirming he heard me with a loud curse, he repeated what I'd just said to Dad and then hung up. "They're on their way. How bad is it?"

With both of our torches now on his face I could see the full extent of the damage to Archer's head. He had a split lip and his nose was bleeding, but it was the large lump on the top of his head with the deep cut in the center that was the biggest worry. I also had a problem.

"Elijah, I need to find her," I rasped, looking up at him desperately. I was torn between making sure my brother was ok and also finding Lottie before he could hurt her badly, or worse – kill her.

The grim look on his face confirmed he had those exact same concerns, too. I'd filled him in on a lot of what had happened since he'd gotten here and he and Lottie had also become good friends, so I knew that he understood what I was going through.

Standing up, he skimmed the beam of his torch across the

ground around us. "There are fresh footprints in the mud over there. I say we follow them until the others catch up with us," he ordered, sounding more like he would if he was at work than he did outside of it. "Uncle Jerome's coming here so he'll look after Archer."

Kneeling down, he turned my brother into the recovery position on his side.

Standing up, I tried to do what I needed to do – remove the emotions making it hard for me to breathe, and think where he could take her. The problem was, there was a lot of land and I didn't know how well he knew it all by now. "What if he has a weapon?"

Pointing for us to go back to the house, he smiled wickedly at me. "So do we."

He was right. We were all good shots – with the exception of Tate, but even then I'd trust him with one tonight – and we knew the land like the back of our hands.

FOLLOWING THE TRACKS ON THE ATVS HADN'T BEEN THAT hard. What had been hard was seeing spots where there were body sized impressions in the ground like he'd dropped her periodically. How much more could one person take? If it had been me I'd have been ok, but Lottie was smaller than I was, she was fragile. Not that I'd tell her that to her face, she'd probably glue my balls to my thigh.

"We're best getting off here," Elijah said quietly as we got closer to the tree line. "The trees are far enough apart to drive through, but if he hears us he might do something to her."

Nodding in agreement, I hopped off the vehicle and walked quietly through the frost-covered grass. It was cold, fucking freezing in fact, and I wasn't sure what sort of clothing Lottie had been in when he took her.

When someone's taken there are the obvious worries, ones that occur to everyone whether they're involved or not. What I hadn't realized until now, though, were the not so obvious ones like what clothing she had on, if she even had shoes and pants on, shit like that. Hypothermia hit quickly, and exposure to a temperature as cold as this with little protecting you from it? Would we find her in time to stop that?

Would we even find her in time to stop him hurting her?

Just then, a body materialized from the trees making me reach for my gun.

"It's only Jackson," Elijah told me, tapping me on the shoulder as he walked past. He was right. Eric Retter was only about five-feet-nine inches tall, but my cousins were all six-foot-four and over. Retter was also built like a weasel in comparison to the big bear standing in front of me right now. "How'd you get here so quickly?"

The night was a clear one and it was a full moon, so I could see his eyes sparkling as he looked in my direction and lifted his chin at me.

"Yo!" Looking back at his brother, he muttered, "Got here about half an hour ago and decided I needed to walk off the journey so I took a wander around. Saw someone headed this way carrying something over their shoulder and figured I'd check it out."

As he spoke, I waited for his twin Marcus to come out of the trees too, but it didn't seem like anyone else was around. "Marcus with you?"

Shaking his head, he turned back to face the direction he'd

come from. "Nah, he had shit to do last night, so we drove separately. Wanna tell me what's going on?"

Waving me forward, Elijah quickly told him what had happened, with Jackson's jaw turning to stone the further into the story he got. He'd known Charlotte's issue with Eric, but hearing the full details and realizing how unhinged he was now, it made things very different.

When he was finished, Elijah motioned for us to start walking. "Story time's over. From now on, we need to be aware, quiet, and sneaky mother fuckers. We don't know what he's carrying, so be ready to defend yourself, ok?"

Defend myself? I wasn't going to defend myself, I was going to fucking kill him.

We'd only been walking for about ten minutes when Noah and Madix joined us, neither of them saying a word. We might not have been trained, but we weren't stupid – we knew what to do.

A rustling to our left sounded as we passed a thick area of bushes, making us all stop and crouch down. Instead of Retter coming out of there, though, Kari appeared.

"What the fuck?" Noah hissed quietly, looking over at me sharply.

Looking back at us, Jackson whispered, "Who's that?"

Pointing at me, Noah replied, "The chick who's been trying to get his attention."

Rolling his eyes, he turned back to watch her as she looked around like she was waiting for someone. Without taking his eyes off her, he held his hand out with his index and middle finger pointing down and started moving them like they were walking. Then, he made the gesture for talking and waved me forward.

Guess I was going to speak to her then. Getting up from my crouch, I walked toward her, calling out, "Kari?"

Spinning around with her hand on her chest, her face went from relaxed to like she was crying. "Levi, oh thank god. I got lost and was so scared."

Making it look like I was searching the area around us, I looked back at where I'd just come from with a look of disbelief on my face. We'd watched her clearly waiting calmly, and what was she doing on our land in the first place?

Turning back to her, I forced a smile onto my face. "Sorry to hear that. If you walk that way, you'll hit the field that leads you down to my parents' house. They can call you a cab."

Before I could turn away from her, she was pulling my arm in the direction I'd told her to go in. "You can't leave me on my own, I might get lost or something. And what if someone finds me? I'm sure I heard footsteps walking past me earlier..."

Tearing my arm out of her grasp and catching her arm instead, I pulled her around to face me. "I'm going to ask you one last time – what are you doing here?"

Nervously licking her lips as her eyes darted around, she stammered, "I wanted to go for a walk, and it's so dark that I... I..."

"You live a long way from here," I snapped, calling her out on her bullshit. "And this is private property, so you're trespassing. Now tell me what the fuck's going on."

I heard the footsteps behind me just before I felt the hand clamp down on my shoulders.

"There're noises in the trees over there, man," Jackson whispered in my ear, and I watched Kari's eyes widen when she saw him. "Tate's coming up on our left, he'll watch this one, we head that way. You with me?"

Not answering, I kept my eyes on her until Tate appeared. "Don't let her out of your sight, man. She's up to something."

"She's involved," Jackson told me, saying out loud what I was already thinking. I wasn't sure how he knew for sure, but her being here was no fucking coincidence.

Not sparing her another glance, I turned and started jogging through the trees behind Elijah. We'd been moving for five minutes when I heard it – the sounds of something being dragged and a deep voice mumbling.

"Could've had it all, but she had to fuck it all up," the voice I recognized as Retter's said, sounding out of it. "Wake up, bitch."

There was a sharp smack and then a low cry followed it. Not thinking, I pushed past my cousin to get to where they were and stop him from hurting her again. Grabbing my arm, he yanked me back and covered his lips with his finger as he shook his head at me and motioned for me to follow him.

Squatting down as low as we could, we used the trees to get to a small bush near where they were, and peeked over the top of it. I'd thought I was struggling before, but the sight in front of me tipped me over the edge.

Lottie was on the floor in a crumpled heap wearing just her jeans and a white t-shirt which was covered in dirt, mud, and blood. Her arms were around her head as she protected the rest of her body with her knees, but there was little strength in her position. A normal person doing that would have their legs tightly up against their stomachs, but hers looked like they were only staying there because she couldn't move them.

"On three," Elijah muttered, pulling his gun out.

Doing the same thing, I braced to move, when another tall figure beat us to it, and grabbed Retter by the neck with one hand then punched him in the stomach with the other.

"Enjoy hurting women, do you?" my cousin Wesley growled, punching him again and dropping him to the floor.

Skidding to my knees beside Lottie, I picked up one of her hands, freaking out when there was no resistance at all.

"Lottie, it's Levi. I've got you, baby."

Jackson jogged up beside me and picked up her other hand, taking her pulse with a frown on his face. "It's weak. Elijah, can you check her over and make sure she's safe to move?"

Dropping to his knees beside me, Elijah started doing his job, all of us ignoring the scuffles going on behind us. "I'm worried about her neck and head, there's no knowing if he dropped her on it. But she needs medical attention ASAP so we're going to have to risk it. Noah's gone to get one of the vehicles and when he gets back, we'll move her. Jackson, support her head and neck."

"Not so fast," a female voice ordered, and we all turned as a woman I didn't recognize walked out of the darkness with a gun pointed at us. "Hands in the air, gentlemen."

Turning to glare at his brother, Elijah snapped, "Really? All of those years you've bragged about nothing getting past you and having the reflexes of a cat, and *that*," he gestured with his thumb over his shoulder, "you didn't see?"

Not looking bothered or moving his hands from where he was supporting Lottie's head, Jackson shook his head. "I saw it."

Wesley stopped hitting Retter as soon as he heard her voice but didn't put his hands in the air either. He did, however, put them on his hips as he watched her walk closer to us.

"I said, put your hands in the air."

Shooting a look of amusement at us, Wesley asked, "Do you want us to wave them around like we just don't care, too?"

"*Say ho-oh!*" Jackson sang, a burst of laughter coming out of him. To anyone else it might look like he genuinely meant it, but his eyes were heated and he wasn't in the slightest bit amused at that moment.

Gaping at us and our failure to comply with her demands, she screeched, "*Hands in the air, I've got a fucking gun.*"

"So do I, lady," Elijah shouted. "In fact, we've all got them. But I'm taking it from how badly your hands are shaking that you don't know how to use one."

In the weeks to come, as I went over tonight's events for the millionth time, I'd think about how we reacted at this moment and realize how stupid we'd been. Whether you believe it's truly dangerous, a gun being waved around isn't anything to laugh at regardless of whether or not you're armed. But right then we were running on anger – and probably arrogance, too – so we didn't give her what she wanted.

Just as he'd said the last word she fired, narrowly missing my head and splintering the wood behind it, pissing us all off even more.

"I told him to make sure he did it when none of you would notice. I told him a thousand times, but he wouldn't listen. Kept taking his drugs and asking if he'd still have his job. Like a doctor can do their job when they're high, the lawsuits would be astronomical and we'd end up broke. But he wouldn't come home without her, so this was the only way to do it. Then I was going to kill him. She's not even mine so what do I care what he does with her, but I won't lose my job and everything I've worked for because of him," she ranted, swinging the gun between all of us. "She's just like Ed, a liability, but the world expects you to get married, expects you to have kids. If I wasn't a family woman, they'd have given the job to someone who was. I've been through too much to fail now."

"Cool story, bro," Jackson yelled to her, still acting unaffected by it. "But it's cold, I need to piss, and I've got cramp in my ass. Wanna get to the point?"

Another shot rang out, this one skimming his arm and making him growl under his breath as the skin opened up.

"Shut up," she screeched, making us all wince involuntarily at the pitch of it.

"She's a fucking whack job," Elijah muttered, unnecessarily telling us something we could all see.

Wesley wasn't close enough to hear it but he turned when Elijah said the words and grinned at us, and then looked back at her. "Are you going to deafen us, or kill us?"

Pointing it at his head this time, she sneered at him. "What do you think? My gun's pointing at your face..."

A large hand appeared over her shoulder, plucking the gun out of hers before she even realized what was happening. And then, in the worst Australian accent I'd ever heard, my cousin Marcus – Jackson's twin – scoffed, "That's not a gun, *this* is a gun." And, walking around in front of her, he held up a Taurus 513. "They call it the Raging Judge, but I prefer the Glock 19 that's in my car."

"You said it all wrong," Jackson called out as the woman's eyes darted between them, no doubt confused why she was seeing double. "It's meant to be a knife. In *Crocodile Dundee*, Mick says that when he shows the dude his knife."

I didn't care if he'd given out the winning lottery numbers, I just wanted to get Charlotte to hospital. Fortunately, Noah and Madix joined us just then, both of them riding an ATV and looking surprised by the appearance of Lottie's mom as well as our other cousin. Even though neither of them questioned it until much later on.

Pushing Raquel Rose down on the ground next to the whimpering shit stain Eric, both Marcus and Wesley stood watching them while we got ready to move Lottie onto the ATV. It was going to be complicated, but we had to make it work. There was no other option.

At least there wasn't until Connor and Barron turned up. Apparently, Noah had texted our dad to let him know exactly where we were, and after they'd cuffed Kari in their vehicle Tate had brought them to us.

Making sure both Raquel and Eric were now unarmed, they radioed through to the EMTs who were waiting for the all clear to approach the area. This meant that we were able to put her onto a stretcher with her neck properly immobilized, before taking her to where the ambulance was.

Now that the threat was gone, and the adrenaline had worn off, it bared mentioning that not one of us was joking or cracking a smile. Far from it. Not that I'd done either of those things once, but even the rest of my family were stony faced and somber as we loaded her into the ambulance and I climbed in beside her. They didn't even crack a joke or try to lighten the mood while we waited for news on her condition at the hospital.

The only purpose that the bantering had served was to keep Kari, Eric, and Raquel off guard. Now we had our full focus on Charlotte.

CHAPTER EIGHTEEN

Charlotte

"You're a disgust," I scolded Rambo, refusing to fall for the sad puppy eyes. "Do you hear me? A dis-gust."

What was his crime? Well, the morning after Eric had taken me almost four weeks ago, Lily and the girls had come up to the house to tidy up and let the guy in to fix the broken window.

They'd seen their box of treats open on the floor in our bathroom still and had rightly figured that I'd move to Peru if anyone else saw them. So they'd boxed it all back up again and had hidden it under the bed – something which they failed to tell us until I accidentally kicked it as I was making the bed a couple of days ago. It would also be pertinent to mention that my bed making abilities consisted of throwing the pillows near the top and pulling up the duvet just now.

I'd pulled it out using my toes, and when I'd recognized the box, I'd put it on the floor in the walk-in closet.

Well, apparently Rambo had found it and we'd walked in to find him using the largest of the training butt plugs as a teething toy. In the middle of the rug. In the middle of the living room. And when I say we, I don't mean Levi and myself, either. The *we* had included Elijah, Webb, Tate, Noah, and Archer, along with Ariana and Bonnie, and not one of them missed what was happening.

And – because that couldn't possibly be bad enough, could it? – just to make it worse, when I'd tried to get it away from him, he'd dragged it behind the couch and had proceeded to play tug-of-war with his brother with it.

"Hey, it's natural to dogs," Webb yawned, totally unphased by it. "They like sniffing butts, so they probably thought it was a bonding thing with you."

Oh my god, kill me now. I'm begging you, just kill me.

Coming to my defense, Levi shot his cousin the bird. "She hasn't used it, asshole."

Grinning at him, Webb drawled, "I'd actually assumed seeing as how it was so easily accessible and the beautiful Charlotte is still all banged up, that it was your personal plug," making everyone burst out laughing.

Shaking his head, he looked over at Noah. "Help me move this thing," he pointed at the couch, "so I can throw that shit away."

Not willing to let it go, Webb got up and helped him instead. "I agree, cousin. Dogs mouths are full of bacteria and with it all chewed up, it would be awkward having to explain how your ass was such a mess if you got an infection because of it."

Giving him a glare, they pulled the couch away from the wall it had been in front of. Sensing that his new toy was about to be stolen, Rambo let out a growl that was probably meant to scare them, but it just sounded like a high pitched trill with the toy between his teeth.

Incidentally, on that couch were two throw cushions that Ariana had given her brother for Christmas with a Daschund on it, and the words *He had a little wiener* written above it. He also had a t-shirt, hoodie, and mug with it on, too. It was hilarious. After I'd left that night, someone had taken a red Sharpie and replaced the a with the number two, and added an s at the end of wieners. Now it read, *He had 2 little wieners*.

"Jesus, look at him go on that thing," Levi chuckled, all of the irritation from seconds away gone as he watched the puppy chewing on it like it was an actual teething toy.

"Maybe they should add that to the packaging? Dog owners could save a fortune in furniture if they got them one of these to chomp on," Webb suggested seriously. "I remember when you got Bogey, Archer, and he ate the leg off the dining table. I thought Aunt Erica was going to shit her pants."

Archer's eyebrows shot up as he looked over the back of the couch. "Hard to believe he can get his tiny mouth around something so big…"

"That's what she said," Elijah snorted, and then took a look himself. "Bogey would have needed the elephant-sized version of one of those."

I wonder if they did those? Not that I wanted one, but now that it had been mentioned I definitely wanted to know if it existed. What was the world's biggest butt plug?

Picking up my phone I typed it in, hoping that no one anywhere in the world had been tasked with watching my internet searches. The results were initially disappointing at

211

five inches high with a fifteen inch circumference. I mean, I wouldn't want to stick one in my own ass, but I'd expected better.

And then I found it. "Holy shit!"

When someone says that as they're looking at their phone, few people can resist either asking or looking, which was proven by Ariana and Bonnie who immediately looked over my shoulder at the screen.

Squinting her eyes, Ariana asked, "What's that?"

"This butt plug is called The Assifier. It's a pacifier for your ass and measures in at thirteen inches long, with a fifteen inch circumference at its widest area," Bonnie read out, then closed her mouth with an audible snap.

There was silence in the room as the three of us read the rest of the description, total forgetting the six men who were now staring at us in a mixture of horror and fascination.

Looking at a photo where it was lying down next to a man's hand, showing the size of the plug, I breathed, "How the hell would you fit that inside you?"

"You're gonna need a lot of lube to stick that sucker in," Bonnie snickered. "We're talking ten sticks of butter up your ass, one of those family sized popcorn buckets worth of lube, and more than likely…"

"Please stop talking," Archer growled, turning stiffly away so that he was looking out the window.

He'd been getting headaches ever since Eric had hit him across the head with a two by four, so immediately I assumed he had another one. "Have you got another headache? Can I get you something for it?"

A loud snort came out of Webb as he looked from his cousin over to us. "Oh, I think his headache will go down in a minute."

His wording confused me, although I guess you could phrase it that way. If a headache or migraine lessened in severity, didn't that mean it had gone down? Something about the way he was laughing quietly and how the other guys mouths were twitching told me my theory was wrong, but without being included in on the joke I didn't know what else to go with.

"Do you need me to massage it?" Bonnie asked, making them laugh even harder. Ever since that night, she'd stopped avoiding him and only giving one-word answers when he spoke to her, and had even helped get him back on his feet.

"I need a second," Elijah wheezed, walking toward the kitchen.

Seeing an escape route, Rambo ran after him, trying to carry the full weight of the plug in his mouth and failing miserably. Before he could get too far, Levi leaned down and grabbed it out of his mouth.

Turning away from it with my cheeks burning all over again, I thought of something to say to distract myself but Ariana got there first. "So, how are you feeling, honey?"

This question wasn't as easy to answer as it seemed. At this moment I was feeling great, regardless of some pain still in different areas of my body. When I was tired that pain increased slightly, a bit like when you're not well and feel worse at night.

Mentally and emotionally I was exhausted, happy, sad, angry, I felt betrayed, I felt loved – I couldn't say that I felt one way because I had too much going on in my head.

And to my shame, I was also horny. Levi wouldn't touch me

until the pain went away, and that was messing with my emotions as well. I also had some paranoia about it in case he didn't want me anymore – which I knew was stupid – or in case he would get tired of waiting for me, which was also stupid.

I didn't want to unload that emotional nightmare onto my friends, though. I was better sorting through it myself. "I still have moments where I'm close to having a panic attack," I explained, angry at one of the other great side effects of what had happened. "If it's dark at night and I can't see, or I'm on my own and hear a noise, that's when the anxiety hits hard. I've had some nightmares but they're starting to get better."

Sighing, Ariana picked up my hand. "And the pain?"

Forcing a smile onto my face, I grinned at her. "It's getting better every day."

A large body kneeling down in front of me almost made me poop my panties, and these were the nice purple ones that Levi liked so much.

Rubbing my thighs with his large hands, Levi didn't take his eyes off mine as he spoke to his sister and Bonnie. "Lottie started talking to a therapist last week about it, and they're going to see each other for a while. It's not going to work itself out overnight, but we're all going to help her."

"I'm in," Ariana agreed, not even taking a second to do it.

Bonnie was the same. "Me too."

Then a chorus of deep voices behind me added, "I'll do it."

The freaking tears that kept appearing out of nowhere built in my eyes, and I was struggling to not let them loose. The support meant everything to me, but I wasn't sure that I wasn't bothering them with this burden.

And Levi, the man had done so much for me, but when was he going to say enough? I hadn't done a damn thing for him, so wasn't that me just using him? What exactly was I bringing to this relationship for him?

Not wanting to share that with everyone, I figured I'd speak to him about it later when they'd all gone home. Until then, I thanked them and let the support and relaxation wash over me.

Just in case, I needed to think of something I could do for Levi. Something special.

Levi

I knew that something was bothering Lottie and given everything that had happened, it didn't surprise me that things reared their heads now and then. It was just getting her to talk about it that was the problem.

I'd just taken the dogs out to go potty and put them in the den with their toys for the night. Ever since that night they hadn't been able to come through to the bedroom in case they jumped on her and hurt her, and she was missing them. It just wasn't worth the pain right now, though. Really, it had only been a matter of taking away the little steps at the end of the bed that she'd bought for them, but she wouldn't have been able to ignore them if they were in the room, so to the den they went.

Leaving the hallway light on in case she needed to go to the kitchen, I strolled into the bedroom and almost tripped over my feet. Kneeling on the edge of the bed, Lottie was wearing a dark blue lace panties and bra set that I hadn't seen before, and she was wearing the necklace I'd bought her for Christmas. It was made of solid silver and was a two inch by two inch copy of the *Flor del Espiritu Santo*, a type of orchid that was Panama's national flower.

I'd been looking for something meaningful online and when I'd seen it described as the dove orchid, I'd seen a lot of Charlotte in the flower. It was beautiful, it was rare, it was unique, it was delicate, but orchids were also robust and resourceful. Doves looked like ordinary birds, but there was something special when they flew up into the skies that made people stare at them and want them for special occasions. She was all of that and more to me, so this necklace was perfect for her.

And it looked amazing nestled between her tits, her pale skin a stark contrast against the shiny silver and the angles of the petals.

The problem wasn't that I didn't want her, because I really, really fucking did. It was torture not being able to slip inside her and take her, having that closeness back. The problem was that she'd been hurt by Eric, and I didn't want to cause her more pain while she continued healing. When I'd found her, it had looked like he'd broken her body into pieces, and we'd all been preparing ourselves for the best case scenario to only be surgeries, casts, and scars.

It sounds ridiculous phrasing that as the best case scenario, but the other scenarios would be ruptured organs, perforated or collapsed lungs, removal of major organs, a traumatic brain injury, paralysis... so really it wasn't that stupid. After doing numerous x-rays, scans, and tests, it was concluded that she'd escaped with severe bruising and exposure to the cold temperature that night. That didn't sound so bad and we were all relieved, but that's because few of us understood exactly how bad bruising could be.

Her right thigh and arm – the side of her body that had been facing up when he'd been beating her – were badly bruised, and the blood had built up in the bruises so badly that they had to put a drain in and were considering surgery at one point.

She'd then developed cellulitis in her thigh as well and had been on IV antibiotics because she'd been so sick with it.

In total, she'd been in hospital for nine days, and had been out of it now for eighteen days. The bruising was beginning to disappear, but there were still dark patches of purple surrounded by yellow over areas of her body.

And I still found her just as beautiful as I had before, and fuck the man card – I loved her even more deeply than I had before.

Pointing at her body self-consciously, she said, "I know I don't look like I did a month ago, but I wanted to show you that I could do things for you, too."

Closing the distance between us, I stood in front of her intending to crouch down, but she stopped me. "Baby, you look as beautiful as you did a month ago."

Sighing, she looked up at the ceiling. "I'm bruised all over and you're having to carry me emotionally and mentally, Levi. You run around doing stuff for me all the time, and I can't do anything for you. That's not a relationship, at least not for us it isn't."

I had to lean down because she was holding my hips now and I didn't want to risk hurting her. She might see it as carrying her, but it was far from that.

Cupping her jaw with my hands, I outlined it for her. Firmly. "Lottie, look at me." When she realized I wasn't going to let her away with not doing it, she looked me in the eye. "I'm not carrying you and this isn't an uneven relationship at all. It's my honor to help you get back to where you were. In the last two months you've been through things that most people – if they're lucky – don't go through even once in their lifetimes. And both times you've tried to continue like nothing's happened, and our minds just don't work that way. Right now you need help, you need someone to support you physically, mentally, and emotionally, and it is an absolute fucking privilege to be the man who does that for you." When the tears started trailing down her cheeks, I moved to kiss her softly. "Don't ever look at it as being an uneven relationship, because you're the one who's carried *me* mentally and emotionally through all of this, too."

"I have?"

I let her see how serious I was and added the words so that she could hear it as well. "I couldn't have gotten through it without you, Lottie."

And that was no fucking exaggeration. I couldn't have. I was in a dark place after that night, one I hadn't been in since Luna had been taken. It had left raw areas inside me that Lottie had healed with everything she did.

Wiping off her cheeks with her hands, she leaned into me. "I want to do more for you."

"More?" What else could she do? She literally gave me everything, there wasn't anything more that I needed from her.

Moving her hands to my ribs, she nudged me to stand up in front of her and reached for the zip of my pants. "I wasn't sure what the best way to do this for a guy was, so I searched online," she admitted, making me burst out laughing.

"Lottie, I don't need you to do this. I'm honestly good with just holding you until you're better."

Yanking my pants and shorts down, she slowly lifted my t-shirt. "I need to do this for you. We're restricted, but we're not totally cut off."

Then her soft hand enveloped my cock and started to move up and down its length, making my legs shake slightly. Pulling my t-shirt off the rest of the way, I threw it behind me as I kicked my pants to the side of the room leaving me totally naked in front of her.

With her free hand, she skimmed her palm up my stomach until she got to my chest, and then she lightly dug her nails in and dragged them back down. Christ, her nails always got me and she knew it.

Gently taking her ponytail and wrapping it around my hand, I pulled her closer to me. "Are you sure?"

Angling my cock up toward her mouth, she paused as she tipped her head back to smile up at me. "I'm going to blow your mind."

And fuck me she did. I'd given her tips on sucking me before she'd gotten hurt, but it had always been as part of our foreplay. Whatever she'd read had gone into shit that I never even knew about.

Keeping her tongue flat, she slowly ran it down the full length of my cock, holding the tip with her hand and raising it up as she got closer to my balls. Once she'd reached them, she started to ascend back up until she got to the top, then dragged a slow swipe over the head.

"Holy shit," I croaked, unable to look away from what was going on. I even begrudged the millisecond it took to blink because I was missing some of it to do it.

Leaning slightly away, she moved her hand down, so that she was now holding it at the base. I want to say that I could predict what she was going to do but there was no urgency in her movements, so it was impossible to tell. She was running the show, and whatever she had going on in her head was how it was going to happen.

Looking up at me, she opened her mouth and slowly enveloped

the tip now, sucking on it as she swiped her tongue across the underneath. Distracted by the sight, I barely registered that one hand was jacking me off with short movements while the other one was now cupping my balls.

Not breaking eye contact, she sank down as far as she could go, and then sucked as she moved back up to the top. Continuing to do this, she also increased the rhythm and speed of her strokes, but just as I got used to it she'd then alternate speeds between her hand and mouth. It was the most complicated thing to describe, the most fucking amazing thing to watch, and fucking outstanding to feel happening all at the same time.

On the next plunge down she moaned hard, her eyes closing like she was the one getting this done not me, and I felt the tingling at the base of my spine. There was a level of etiquette to getting a blow job – not to be a selfish asshole. You needed to warn the woman, not assume that it was ok to just blow.

My head fell back on my neck and I tried to do just that. "Lottie." When she ignored it and continued to descend, I went a step further. "Baby, I'm going to come."

Moving the hand that wasn't helping her mouth so that it was around my hip, she dug her nails in and pulled me in to her. The tingle intensified to a full on electric shock and I exploded, coming in pulses in her mouth as I lost the feeling in my arms and legs. Hell, at this stage, I didn't even have any other parts of my body, they'd all disappeared as it swept through me leaving a panting, shaking wreck behind.

When I couldn't take anymore, I pulled out of her mouth and stared down at her in shock. The skin of her chest now had goosebumps all over it and her hard nipples were poking through the lace, making me realize how much this had affected her to.

I might not be able to make love to her, but I could give her back what she'd just given me, regardless of the fact it worried her that she was the only one receiving in this relationship.

Pointing behind her, I growled, "Lie out on the bed, now."

And then I blew her mind, too. Twice.

CHAPTER NINETEEN

Charlotte

*S*ix months later...

Life was good – I hated that expression because it was so weak. My life wasn't just good, it was so much more than that.

Eric was charged and had been sentenced to fifteen years in prison yesterday. His withdrawals had apparently been the stuff of nightmares, and seeing as how he hadn't been granted bail, he'd had to go through it in prison. One of the guards who was friends with Connor had told us that he'd seen a lot of men go through it, but not one of them had been as bad as that. Levi's reasoning was because he was a 'pussy assed bitch' and no one had argued with that.

My mom had been granted bail, but they had also given me a restraining order while she was waiting to go to trial, so that wasn't a big issue. She was definitely going to get a sentence too, seeing as how she'd helped a wanted person kidnap me knowing that he intended to hurt me.

The only shock had been when it came to Kari. While he was being questioned, Eric had explained how she'd approached him outside the bar the night we were in there and had offered to help him kidnap me. Her father was about to be indicted for fraud and embezzlement, so she wanted money to fall back on – Levi's.

He might have been high as a kite but he'd had the sense to record most of the conversation, including the part where she'd told him to do whatever he wanted with me. My favorite part had been her saying, "Kill the little bitch for all I care." Hairy assed, man footed cow.

And my father… maybe it was best that I didn't tackle that subject. This was meant to be a happy day for me, and his disregard was the one thing in the whole debacle that actually hurt me.

When he'd been told what Raquel had been part of, he'd replied with a simple, "Ok." Eventually, Levi had called him and outlined the plan, including details of my injuries, and he'd just muttered another, "Ok," and had hung up the phone. I hadn't heard from him or seen him, and I didn't want to ever again.

Aside from that, life really was good. Levi's family, including his cousins and grandparents, were amazing, and I never knew what to expect with them. *Forrest Gump*'s mama totally got it wrong in her analogy about boxes of chocolates. It was true that you never knew what you were gonna get, but if you dug out the ones that people automatically went for – the run-of-the-mill flavors that were common everywhere – all you were left with were the nuts.

And the Townsends were my nuts. Maybe I needed to reword my analogy, too? Then again, I loved nuts, so being left with a variety of them because everyone preferred the boring, normal ones was perfect for me.

I'd also decided not to stop my bucket list. I was now about to turn twenty-two, and my twenty-first year had definitely been full of life changes, but I didn't want to quit experiencing things I wouldn't normally.

Which was why Levi had arranged for me to go bungee jumping at The Sierra Nevada Mountains Bridge, a railway bridge that ran between the mountains next to Lake Tahoe. I'd been pumped until we'd gotten to the area where you jumped off, and then the nerves had set in.

Giving myself a pep talk had worked, and then I'd looked down at the hundred foot drop. Needless to say, I wasn't ok right now.

Massaging my shoulders, Levi murmured, "You don't have to do this, Lottie. We can find one of those kids adventure parks, or go to one of those places where you stand in a big tube and they blow a lot of air to lift you up."

"Ok, Charlotte," Craig the jump guy yelled. "You're next."

With a whimper, I walked over to him and stepped into the harness.

"Do you remember what we went through in the safety briefing?" Darnell, the other bungee guy asked.

Nodding at him, I closed my eyes and thought of my happy place. On the ground. On firm ground with concrete boots on my feet. Not standing roughly one hundred feet above the water with a piece of string around my torso, some elastic around my ankles, and a GoPro being attached to me.

"Step up to the edge, Charlotte," Craig instructed while

Darnell checked all the clasps on the equipment that I'd just been strapped into.

Maybe he should do that before I stepped closer to the drop?

When he was happy, he gave a thumbs up and grinned at me. "Are you ready?"

Fuck no! "Yes."

"Lottie," Levi called, making me jump.

Looking over my shoulder, I saw him on one knee holding out a small box with something shining in it.

I'm not sure if it was the nerves of the jump or the shock of what I saw, but I tripped and went flailing off the edge of the bridge, screaming my ass off the whole way.

I was still screaming as I hurtled to my death, when I blinked my eyes open for a brief second and saw a crowd of people waving at me out of the corner of my vision, but my life was about to end and I was going at such a fast pace that I'd never know who was saying goodbye to me.

As the water rushed up at me, I closed my eyes and felt a second of heartbreak that I'd never get to marry Levi and wear the ring he'd picked for me.

Just as I was taking my last breath, I hit the end of the elastic and string – or the very safe and professional harnesses, but I wouldn't look at them like that until at least a week later – and my internal organs felt like they'd shifted into my breasts. Then I was shooting back up again, then falling, continuing on like that until I finally stopped completely.

That was the first time I fully opened my eyes all the way and saw how far away from the water I was. Facing it, it didn't seem like that far, but when I saw the photos afterwards there had been a distance of at least ten feet.

Hearing cheering to my right, I turned my head and saw all the Townsends – all of them – standing cheering and clapping. Well, aside from Levi who had somehow joined them and was standing next to his parents, Elijah, and his grandmother, all of them looking like they were about to drop dead.

The GoPro thankfully recorded everything I'd missed, including the expression on my face when I saw Levi and tripped off the edge, so I got to see it. Some of the family had also recorded or photographed it as well, so I had those to add to it, too.

Which was just as well – because I was never doing it again. Ever!

The one part I wanted to relive a million times over, though, was Levi scooping me up when I got closer to him and putting the ring on my finger without saying a word.

Regardless of the fact that I was still shaky, I burst out laughing. "Is that your idea of a proposal?"

Scowling up at the bridge and then back down at me, he shook his head seriously. "A proposal involves asking if you're marrying me, and that means you can say no, so I'm not asking. You will marry me, and you're never doing anything that fucking stupid again."

WANNA KNOW WHY HE WAS AS SHAKEN AS HE WAS BY IT ALL? Well, I'd found out later on that Levi had set it up, thinking he'd be able to propose and that I wouldn't jump. He knew how afraid of heights I was, but wanted me to have the opportunity to attempt it, regardless. He just hadn't counted on me actually going over the edge. Darnell and Craig had been in on it, too, but the proposal was the real reason why the whole family were there that day.

Levi's plan was to get me ready, and then for him to do what he'd done and me to fall into his arms. Nowhere in there did I end up over the edge, so it was just as well they had strapped me into the harness.

As I'd tripped over the edge, there was a clear video of all them trying to catch me and missing by an inch. There was also a nice close up of Levi's horrified expression as I continued falling. It felt like it had all been over in a matter of seconds, but the fall had lasted long enough for him to get all the way to his family, see that I was ok, and almost throw up in the bushes.

At least we had the best videos and photos to show our kids and grandkids – if we ever had them – of the day he proposed. That reasoning would come in handy once the shock wore off, but I was totally getting myself concrete boots.

IRONICALLY, THREE MONTHS LATER, HE ASKED ME TO MARRY him again. This time we were on vacation at Guadalupe Island in Mexico, cage diving with sharks, and this adventure had been my surprise for him.

We'd flown into San Diego and met our ship which had then brought us here, and now we were in a cage looking out into the dark blue depths of the water around us. I'd expected it to be crystal clear, but it was like being in a weird clear, yet murky, blue soup, and we couldn't see what was in the distance ahead or below the cage.

It was eerie, and I wasn't sure that us watching *47 Meters Down* and *The Meg* last week had been a good idea. Levi had wanted to have a shark day, though, and I hadn't wanted to give away what the surprise was, so I hadn't had a choice.

Let me just say that if you could smell fear in water – mine would be enough to knock you out right now.

Wait, sharks could, though, couldn't they?

A tap on my shoulder almost made me shit my pants, and when I turned to look at Levi he was holding up a board with:

> *No heights this time.*
> *Will you marry me?*

Followed by the words yes and no with boxes beside them.

Just as I reached out to tick yes, the expression on his face turned to one of horror as he stared behind me, and then something hit the cage.

Turning around as fast as I could, I saw the open mouth of a Great White only feet away from my face and screamed. Well, I would have screamed if I hadn't had the vital scuba breathing regulator mouthpiece in my mouth. Still, I gave it my best shot, and bubbles exploded around it as the shark ran his teeth down the bar of the cage.

Ironically, there were also GoPros in the cage with us, recording the moment for us to relieve again, and again. They also recorded the explosion of bubbles from the front and behind. Yes, behind. The video showed Levi reacting much the same way that I did, except from the opposite end of his body.

At least we survived another memorable proposal, and the video footage to show for it.

EPILOGUE

L evi was still trying to give me the proposal of my dreams up until last night, one where nothing went wrong. He'd tried so many ways to make it work, but nothing had gone right.

Now, we had a long list of proposals to fall back on when we told the story of how he proposed, but I wasn't going to stop at just telling one of the stories.

We'd gone back to see one of the football teams who'd been playing during that fateful game, but one of the guys on the cameras had recognized us, and as his proposal flashed up on the screen, it had cut to me looking like I was jacking him off as I dried his crotch.

Then, a couple of weeks after the football game, he'd organized a ride on Night Rider and his Dad's horse, but something had spooked it and Levi had fallen and broken his tailbone. Jer's horse's name was Senegal Heat, but they called him SH and swore it stood for Shit Head. Now I could see why.

The list was endless, and each one had ended as badly as the one before it.

"Why are you giving her so many chances to say no?" Archer had asked as we'd waited the night he'd fallen off SH, next to Levi's hospital bed for Parker to come back with the results of the x-ray.

Slightly out of it with the painkillers he'd been given, he'd slurred, "I want to give her all of her dreams."

And that's when he'd given me the proposal of my dreams without even realizing it. He'd still continued trying, though, but I had all that I ever needed and more.

Levi

It was done, she was legally all mine. Her signature was on the piece of paper and I'd gone over everything ten times to make sure nothing had been missed out. Even filing the paperwork for the marriage license, I'd checked it over, woken up at two in the morning to check it again, and had fallen back to sleep with it in my hand in case it disappeared.

But it had all gone without a hitch, and now she was mine for the rest of my life. Her and her sexy thigh socks – which she still wore to bed during the winter. Admittedly, I'd bought her at least five pairs of the things in September to make sure she had enough, but the whole Charlotte and sexy thigh socks package was all mine.

I hadn't realized that breaking my ass would mean waking up to the happiest Charlotte I'd ever seen, but apparently the words I'd slurred out had been all that she'd needed.

Technically, the first time I'd proposed had been all she'd needed, but I'd kept doing it because I was desperate to not have a failed one for her to remember. Not that you could forget the others, especially because of all the damn videos and photos we now had of all of it. Fucking technology.

Walking past where my sister was reluctantly dancing with Parker, I frowned when I saw how closely he was holding her.

"Yo," I barked, wedging my arms between them and pushing him away slightly. "Leave space for Jesus, man."

I was insanely happy, but the glare he was shooting at me just added to it.

Now to find my wife.

Charlotte

ONE YEAR LATER...

"Bop, bop, bop!"

Putting my milkshake down on the table, I turned and glared at Ariana. "Stop poking my vagina."

"I'm not poking your vagina, I'm poking the baby's foot."

Shooting a pleading look at Bonnie and Dahlia, I sighed when they just shrugged at me.

"I'm thirty-nine weeks pregnant and at the last appointment with my OB-GYN, she said his head was in the 'good to go' position. So that wouldn't be his foot even if it wasn't my vagina. Which," I added, leaning closer to her face, "it is."

Looking horrified, she cried, "Oh my god, what if I got him in the eye?"

"They just do a scan up your cooter at the eye doctor," Dahlia told her seriously, pulling out her phone. "Here, I'll make an appointment."

Seeing how flustered I was getting, Bonnie plucked it out of her hand. "Let's not wind up the pregnant woman, ladies. She might explode all over us."

"Explode?" Ariana gasped.

"I won't explode, and you weren't poking him in the eye," I reassured her, but couldn't help adding, "because you were poking my vagina."

Unfortunately, as I was saying those last six words, the McDonalds we were sitting in went unnaturally quiet, so everyone heard them and turned to look at us.

"I wanna watch," a big guy in a red cap yelled, scooting around in his chair so he didn't miss the show.

"Me too," another voice shouted, which was soon followed by three more.

Feeling indigestion weaseling its way back into my day, I threw my garbage on my tray and stood up. One by one, the eyes of the men who'd called out to us dropped to the large bulge of my stomach - which was impossible to miss so I didn't take any offense at them doing this, especially seeing as how there was a leg sticking out of it at that moment.

"Mommy," a little boy whimpered, launching himself at the woman beside her. "She's got an alien in her belly." Giving me a sympathetic smile, she whispered something to him that just made it worse. "I'm not eating here then, I don't want an alien in my belly."

Shaking his head, red cap turned back to his meal, but said loudly over his shoulder, "Just to say, I'd still watch."

"You're a sick man," Bonnie growled at him. "I'll give you a tip: get yourself a woman, treat her like a queen, and then you won't need the big vat of lube you've got waiting for you at home."

Looking her up and down, he shrugged. "I'd give you more than the tip. You'd get the whole foot long."

Wrinkling her nose, she muttered, "Gross," at the same time that I started gagging.

"Wrong restaurant, phlegm wad," Dahlia called, shaking her head and pointing at the golden arches outside the window.

Feeling the pain in my stomach building, I shot Ariana a begging look and started walking slowly toward the front door of the restaurant.

Just as I got to the door, there was a gush of water between my legs and I had to grab onto the handle to stop myself falling to the floor with the pain.

"We've got to go," I whimpered, trying to pull the door toward me to open it. "I'm not having my baby in here. I'm having him in a sterile bed, in a sterile hospital, with my husband beside me, *where there's drugs!*" The last word came out on a shriek as I tried my hardest to get the damn door to open, but it just wasn't budging. "Oh god, he's gonna be called Mac, isn't he?"

Pushing the door beside the one I was still pulling on, Ariana suggested, "Or you could call him nugget?"

With their help, I made it to Levi's truck. Then, with the help of Archer, who had been driving past at that moment, I made it into the truck – which was the biggest miracle. Levi could have attached an elevator for the last three months of this pregnancy, and I still would have struggled to get in and out of the thing. Fortunately, him being there meant he could call Levi and my OB-GYN as he tried to get the seatbelt around my girth.

"If you say it doesn't fit, I'll shove a watermelon up your ass," I growled, panting through the latest contraction.

Biting back a laugh, he said into the phone, "Yes, that's your delicate flower. Oh, she's just fine, don't you worry. This is going to be the most memorable experience of your life." Then he paused and looked at his sister, a grin I hadn't seen a lot of on his mouth. "Say, do you have your phone fully charged? You need to record the birth for her so she can see the beautiful wonders of nature."

Melting at his words, the true meaning of them lost on me, I sighed, "Aw, Archer, that's so sweet. You're my favorite you know."

Turning the key in the ignition, the engine rumbled to life at the same time that Ariana flicked me on the side of the head. "Hey, I'm sitting right here."

Almost like we were in a movie, Levi pulled into the parking lot and stopped right beside us. With the engine still running, he got out of the car and ran over to my door, pushing his brother out of the way.

"Are you ok? Where does it hurt?"

There was a thud and a beep of the horn as Ariana's head dropped down onto the steering wheel. "I'm surrounded by imbeciles."

Losing patience with it all, Bonnie and Dahlia got out of the back and walked around to join Levi and Archer at my door.

"Where do you think it hurts, Levi? She has a baby the size of a calf about to explode out of her vagina," Dahlia snapped, pushing Archer to the side and reaching out for my hand, just as another contraction hit on the back of the previous one. "Um, they're really close together, Charlotte."

If I hadn't been feeling what I felt now, I wouldn't have said what I did next. "It feels like I need to poop, like now. It's like a huge torpedo's been launched."

Shooting a nervous look at Ariana and nodding at whatever she did back, Dahlia asked, "Is it as bad as the biggest plug?"

I didn't know, I'd never made it that far into the training kit. In fact, I'd managed plug number two in the lineup and had almost had to call for help when I couldn't get it back out. Incidentally, that was the day I realized exactly how squeamish Levi was when it came to poop, and I got to call him a liar for saying he'd help me explore the dirtier side of sex with me. Not that I was disappointed, but my ass was going to remain a one-way street. Well, unless this kid ripped it open, and then it was going to be an interstate.

Groaning, I leaned back so that my back was across the length of the bench seat and my head was in Ariana's lap.

"There's a lot of pressure. Oh, shit the size of a truck! It was only five nuggets, why is it so bad?"

"Parker says you need to check her vagina," she yelled at the group by my feet, making all of them take a step away from where they'd just been.

When no one stepped back to do it, I screamed, "Stop being pussies and look at my vagina!"

It was uncharacteristic for me, sure, but I was scared, I was in pain, and this wasn't how it was supposed to go. More pregnancies and labors went right than wrong, but some still went wrong, and I was terrified something would happen to my son.

I still suffered from PTSD and flashbacks of the night Eric had taken me so I hadn't been able to get my CNRN yet, but on the whole I was doing well - at least I had been until I'd found out that I was pregnant. After that, all the anxiety and worry had transferred onto the baby I was carrying and whether or not they'd be ok, so having it in a truck in a parking lot was bringing on an anxiety attack of epic proportions.

"I'll do it," a deep voice called out, one that was familiar but I just couldn't place it.

"Fuck off, red cap," Bonnie hissed, and I blushed at knowing that the pervert was right there.

The anxiety I'd just been feeling was taken over by anger that he was making my precious moment dirty. "Go shove a baseball bat up your ass, you dirty pervert. This is a beautiful moment, and I…" I broke off on a scream as something set my poor cooch on fire.

"Will one of you check her damned vagina," Ariana yelled, losing patience now. "You need to be ready to catch the baby if he comes out."

So, with Archer's back to us, red cap long gone, and Bonnie doing her best not to faint, Dahlia brought my son Niklaus into the world, and passed him to his daddy. He was still attached to his mommy at that moment, so Levi had to step up close to me.

We'd decided on Niklaus because Elijah was going to be his godfather, and as we'd been watching The Originals one night, I'd come up with the idea of pairing the names of the two Mikaelson brothers together. Levi had been surprisingly enthusiastic about it, but when we'd told Elijah he'd burst out laughing thinking that we were joking.

Not about the name, mind you, about him being the godfather. Spoiler alert for him, we weren't.

⌒‒‒‒‒

Read on for news in the note that follows. M xox

LOVE, MARY X

Each character that I write is different. Although some of the backgrounds might be similar, the personalities never are. Whenever I start a book, I have to spend some time thinking about the characters first, remind myself about the other ones personalities, and then figure out exactly how I want them to be inside. It's not a quick process, but it means that I can understand them all better – especially if it's a Townsend. Those guys are crazy, they're deep, they all have their own quirks, and they're a blast to write. I also fall in love with them quickly.

Why am I telling you this? Well, I knew who Levi was – especially after Until Fools Find Gold – and I knew how I wanted him to be. But I can absolutely confirm that I didn't expect him to turn out to be a spanky alpha. Until now, Cole and Tate have always been my favorite Townsends, there was just something 'special' about the two of them. Now, though, it is absolutely Levi (and Cole, obviously).

I'll also never be able to listen to *Inside* by Stiltskin again without blushing – thank you, Levi.

It's been a big year for the Townsends and Providence Gold, and I just want to take this opportunity to thank all of you for your support, your patience, your awesomeness, and to wish all of you the very best for 2020.

Merry Christmas, guys, and I hope you have a wonderful time.

M xox

PS. *Oh, and if you didn't guess by the appearances in the book… the Providence Family Ties series starts in 2020, too. And these aren't your normal Townsends, hell no. The Townsend-Rossi family are dark, they're deep, they're dirty, but they're also Townsends so we can't erase that from their stories completely. But it's a whole new breed of Townsends that starts next year!*

ABOUT THE AUTHOR

I'm a British author who grew up all over the world. My parents were diplomats, so we were posted to all of the corners of the earth and it was a *blast*. Some wouldn't seem so awesome if you heard about them, but my parents always made it a fun experience and it molded my brother and I into who we are today.

I live in Wiltshire in the west country of the UK. At random times of the day, I'll hear a moo from the fields around me, or get a whiff of that...uhhh...'country air', and I love it! I might not have grown up in the UK, but I'm a British girl to the bone (regardless of the suspicious whiffs coming in from the fields).

I'm a single mother with a son who is nearing his teenage phase. Maybe he's reached it early? Who knows. But he's awesome and has a personality and sense of humor that I can only attribute to my family. We're slightly bonkers, we have a wicked sense of humor and we find the positives in every situation. I'm so proud to be his mum and to watch him grow and mature.

Writing was something that I'd always done. I had a teacher in the third grade who always set us the task of writing a story and making it into a book every weekend. After I left school, I kept this up and wrote as often as I could or just plotted out books. This evolved into me taking the plunge and publishing my first book in 2016 and I've been typing ever since.

I'm proud to be an Indie Author, and I absolutely love writing out my crazy Providence characters and the more complex ones in my other series'. It doesn't matter if it's romantic comedy or something with more suspense – so long as it has a HEA I'll do it!

I've got so many more planned, so the best is yet to come.

Want to hear more about upcoming releases and hear from characters from the Providence and Providence Gold Series? Sign up to my newsletter:

https://landing.mailerlite.com/webforms/landing/n6g2k1

Wanna join in on the crazy unicorn loving tainted romance shenanigans? Come and join my group on Facebook, 50 Shades of Neigh!

https://www.facebook.com/groups/144042859588361/

PROVIDENCE GOLD SERIES BOOKS

Until Fools Find Gold - Noah and Luna

Mad Gold - Madix and Dahlia

Tainted Gold - Tate and Lily

Going For Gold - Levi and Charlotte

Forbidden Gold - Parker and Ariana

Heart of Gold - Archer and Bonnie

Visit Amazon to see my other books including the original
Providence Series and Cheap Thrills.

Printed in Great Britain
by Amazon

21530695R00148